MW00618521

VENGEANCE

A Crime Novel

Jake Jacobs

ISBN 978-1-62806-363-9   (print | paperback)

Library of Congress Control Number 2022920665

Published by Salt Water Media
29 Broad Street, Suite 104
Berlin, MD 21811
www.saltwatermedia.com

Cover art by Tobie Jacobs

Vengeance

CONTENTS

AUTHOR'S NOTE

I was a cop for thirty years and a detective for almost all of those. I've carried a gun for over fifty years and still do. To say I saw a lot of bad stuff would be an understatement. I met some dangerous people and was happy to play a part in putting a lot of them behind bars where they belonged. I also met a lot of good people who helped me and influenced me throughout my career.

Rather than tell you a story about a specific case, I have merged memories of many cases into the telling of a single story.

This is a fictional crime story drawn from real life and seen through the eyes of a police officer made cynical by years of being on guard and not trusting many people.

Life is hard and seldom fair. Innocent people are hurt every day by criminals who prey upon the weak and unsuspecting.

Never let your guard down. Even when you're in a peaceful beach town in the dead of winter, bad shit can happen.

Have you ever been to Sandpiper?

1

PEGGY - DECEMBER 2020

It was getting colder and darker than Peggy thought it would be, but she knew it was her fault for getting a late start. Running on the beach every day after work was her release, her way of keeping focused and in shape. It was mid-December, but the weather had been unusually mild, and her sweat pants and hoodie were keeping her warm as her feet beat a steady rhythm on the wet sand. She always ran in wet sand because it was firmer; she had sprained her ankles running in soft sand too many times. She knew she should turn around and go back because if she ran her entire five miles, she would be returning in total darkness. She was alone on the beach and as the sun set, the only light she had was the glow from some of the taller condominiums lining this portion of the beach. All the other joggers had gone in long ago, already populating the pubs and clubs that occupied Ocean Highway, or were on their way to get ready to work the evening shifts at any number of resort businesses. Workers eked out a living during the off months of winter.

She could kick herself for staying the extra hour at work,

but she was dedicated, and when the administrative judge of the District Court asks you to do him a favor, you just can't say no and go home. It was Tuesday, so nothing else was going on. Running in the dark did not scare her; she had grown up in this town and had always felt safe. It was especially so in the wintertime when all the crazies were back in the big cities.

The sound of waves breaking a short distance away helped ease the stress of the day and had always been part of the attraction of running on the beach. Peggy couldn't imagine a better place to be or a more compelling reason to live on the shore.

Where the ocean had receded Peggy could just make out footprints of someone who had preceded her on the beach. The footprints were faint and had obviously been covered by the surging and receding waters several times, but not too often because they were still there. Judging by the size, it was probably a man, but sand was a funny thing and often left impressions that were distorted. Peggy ran for another quarter mile, following the footprints as if they were a road map to her future. No one else was on the beach; she heard nothing other than the breaking waves. It was a dark, cloudy night that blocked out most of the reassuring light of the moon.

Suddenly the footprints she had been following weren't there anymore. Had they turned toward the water or towards the hotels and condominiums? Peggy wasn't tired, but she stopped because the sudden disappearance of the footprints didn't make sense. With total darkness quickly approaching, Peggy examined the sand more closely and became even more confused by the fact that it looked like someone had raked away the footprints. She turned to look at the dark waves rolling into to the shore in never-ending sets. Nothing to see there, but as she began to turn towards the buildings, she had an overwhelming feeling she was no longer alone.

The hand that covered her mouth felt like it was gloved; she could feel another hand encircle her waist and begin pulling her down. Peggy was in shape from running, but had no skills in self-defense. She had never been confronted with danger before. Her mind froze and it was like she was watching things occur to her from an out-of-body experience.

Peggy's "fight-or-flight" came to her as she kicked violently, trying to disengage herself from her attacker. Too little, too late! She felt her strength and her life begin to slip irreversibly from her. She felt a helplessness like never before and a fear overwhelming all her other senses. *Would Judge Nelson realize his request for a favor had sentenced her to death?* she thought. *Probably not.*

A burning sensation began to register in her side and she couldn't figure out how a hand could inflict such sharp pain—unless it was holding a knife. *Oh God, no!*

It was happening just like he had been taught. The hoodie provided no resistance to the knife as it slid easily through her skin and between her ribs. He stopped for a split second, but then buried the knife to its hilt. Without pulling it out he wiggled it so the tip would be moving within her body, creating the ultimate amount of damage to every organ it touched. Lonnie's training in Marine Corps techniques, while he was he jail, had kicked in and he was on cruise control. The upside to serving time was you always came out harder and smarter than when you went in. Prison is like graduate school for criminals.

Her pain seemed to grow unbearable—then there was no pain. There was no light. There was no thought. There was no life. Peggy died on Sandpiper's Beach.

It may have helped Peggy in her final moments had she known she was his first and had been dispatched quickly. The future would be far less kind to other women who viewed this beach community as a haven of fun and adventure.

As he lowered her to the sand he whispered in her ear, "Who's laughing now?" If she heard him she was beyond response.

The time was 5:45 p.m., Tuesday, December 11th. Peggy's body temperature would soon match the temperature of the cold, wet sand upon which she laid.

2
LONNIE – JULY 2010

The town of Sandpiper is located on Maryland's Atlantic shore. Because it is a beach community, the name Sandpiper Beach has become interchangeable with its legal name.

It was the middle of the 2010 summer season in Sandpiper Beach. It had started off innocent enough when he began hitting on a blond girl he met on the boardwalk that fronts the ocean between 1st and 13th Street in Sandpiper. Like all boys his age, Lonnie Harris, who had just turned 17 — was looking to get laid, and this pretty little thing was pressing all the right buttons. She said her name was Gerri and she was visiting with her parents. She told him she lived in Rockville, Maryland, and they came down for a week every year. Her best girlfriend was supposed to come with them, but had canceled just days before the trip, not giving her enough time to find another friend to bring to the beach.

At the time, Lonnie was a skinny little blonde himself. He was pale by local standards and ventured onto the beach only when it suited his needs. His needs usually revolved around watching the scantily clad teenage girls or scoring some dope from local dealers who hung out on the beach. At 5'8" and 140 pounds, Lonnie did not present a very threatening figure.

Apparently, the lonely blonde from Rockville thought he would do in a pinch; she liked the way he seemed to be drooling at her budding breasts filling her new bikini.

They talked about school and how they both hated it and couldn't wait to be on their own. Both lied about where they had been and how they ran wild and did what they wanted despite attempts by their parents to restrict them. Lonnie didn't have to lie much because his mother never knew where he was and didn't seem to care. She worked two jobs and as long as Lonnie wasn't bringing the law or school authorities to her doorstep, she was okay with him doing his thing. Lonnie had never met his dad and knew only that he had not stayed around long enough to see Lonnie born. Lonnie suspected he was one of the local waterbilly's who worked the fishing or crabbing boats. Lonnie didn't care. One less person to give him shit.

It was late in the afternoon before Gerri said she had to go back to her parent's rental unit or she would get in real trouble. By now, Lonnie had such a raging hard-on, he begged her to stay with him. He promised he would score some dope and they could go down to the sand and get high. Gerri seemed to like the idea, but said she had to have dinner with her parents; then she could come out and stay until about 10 p.m. She told Lonnie she was sixteen years old, but her parents were very strict. Later Lonnie would learn she had just turned fourteen. Lonnie knew it wouldn't have mattered if she said she was twelve. He was going to get some of that blonde girl. She was hot and he was ready. They struck a deal to get together again at 7:00 p.m. at 9th Street and the boards.

Not wanting to miss this opportunity, Lonnie was in place at 6:30. At 7:15 he was becoming agitated as he scanned the many young girls moving up and down the boardwalk. Lonnie had made so much headway with Gerri, he did not want to start again with some other dumb chick that would lead him on and then run when things started to turn serious. With Gerri he knew he had a chance—if he could just get her alone. At 7:20 Gerri came tearing up to Lonnie and threw her arms around him. "I'm so sorry I'm late. My parents took so long to eat dinner and I couldn't leave until they were done." She received instant forgiveness as the blood began to engorge Lonnie's penis.

Lonnie had been true to his word and had scored a little bit of weed. He had a six-pack of beer he had stolen from his mother's refrigerator. He would make it up to his mom later. Not really, he considered her a stupid drunk, whom would never miss six beers.

The beer had been iced in a beach bag from his house. The sun disappeared over the bay around 8:00 giving Lonnie approximately two hours to work his magic.

When you get past 13th Street the boardwalk ends and is replaced with dunes adorned with different types of sea grass to keep them in place. Because city landscapers want the dunes to look natural, they are placed randomly and overlapping along the beach. The dunes create their own little nooks and crannies that young lovers have taken advantage of for as long as there have been dunes. At night you would literally have to trip over someone to find them in the dunes. This particular night there was almost a full moon and it gave light to some of these secret hideaways.

Lonnie was well versed in these hiding places. He took

Gerri to one of his favorites where you could even light up a joint and not be seen from the beach or from the buildings. Very private. Perfect.

Gerri wore short shorts and a blouse purposely unbuttoned at the top. When she left her parents, it was buttoned to the top, but she wanted to show everyone that she was not a little girl anymore. After two beers each and a shared joint, they began the ritual of making out. Lonnie was patient, but not too patient. Holding hands led to kissing. Kissing led to touching the outside of each other's clothing, and then Lonnie slid his hand inside the welcoming opening at the top of her blouse.

Her nipples were erect and so was he. Lonnie began pulling at the remaining buttons on her blouse with one hand and trying to undo the front of her shorts with his other hand. Things were moving fast; Gerri decided maybe too fast. She pulled his hand from her breasts and tried to catch her breath so she could tell him to slow down. She had never been all the way with a boy, but she didn't want to admit how inexperienced she really was. She was even less experienced in stopping this fast-moving train. Lonnie was not to be denied at this point, so he pushed Gerri down into the sand. He covered her with the weight of his own body while he continued to fondle her. He removed the thin pieces of fabric that kept him from his goal.

The struggle was picking up intensity when Lonnie realized he had let his imagination out pace his actual progress. He tried to stop. He tried to pull back and neutralize his thoughts. Too late; he felt the spasms as he ejaculated inside his own pants. Bad enough that he had a premature ejaculation, but he was wearing thin tan shorts and his situation would become very clear to anyone looking at, or feeling, that area.

Gerri realized what had happened because she had seen other boys in similar circumstances. She always thought it was funny when they got carried away and presented the evidence for the world to see. She laughed at Lonnie and felt a sense of relief that he would probably stop now and let her leave rather than face further embarrassment.

Lonnie had many faults, but at the top of the list was his hatred of being laughed at. Because he was a small boy, this was a frequent occurrence among his peers. Even his mother laughed at him at inappropriate times. He hated her when she did it.

Now he hated Gerri and would not let some out-of-town bitch go home with a great story of how she had made some surf bum cum in his own pants. No, he would get what he wanted. He knew his erection would return shortly and he intended to use it appropriately when it did.

Lonnie pushed Gerri down in the sand with a new fury that scared her. She began to struggle in an effort not only to stop him, but to get away. She started to scream. He silenced her with a vicious slap across the face. While she was still stunned he pulled hard on her blouse, trying to rip the buttons off. They held fast and he remembered the small three-inch pocket knife he always carried in his pocket. He held her in place with his forearm while he opened the knife. Lonnie quickly cut away at her blouse. The knife found purchase in more than fabric. It cut into Gerri's skin and blood was soon flowing from multiple small cuts on her breasts and neck area. Now she really did scream and in reaction to that scream Lonnie struck out at her face with his pocket knife. Blood was everywhere, but Lonnie continued to hack at Gerri's clothes with little regard to the damage he was doing to her body. She was nude and he was inside her. He didn't last long. Passion and anger merged and he was wasted.

Gerri laid still. Lonnie began to think about what had happened, and how badly it would end for him. Lonnie imagined being arrested and losing his freedom. He thought, *it was her fault. She made me do it, but nobody will believe me or understand why I had to kill her.* Lonnie did the only thing he could think of at the time — he plunged the knife into her chest again and again until he was sure she was dead. Nobody knew they were together. Nobody would ever know what really happened here. Lonnie was in a state of panic, but he knew he had to flee. He got up, dropping his knife in the sand, and ran into the ocean, ridding himself of the blood that now spattered his clothes, hands, and face. He moved down the coast. When he was convinced the blood and cum had been washed away, Lonnie reentered the beach and then the boardwalk where he was observed as just another crazy teenager who had gone swimming in his clothes.

Back in the dunes Gerri stirred. The pain was everywhere. She knew she was badly hurt and needed help. She summoned up all her strength and began screaming. Her hand touched the bleeding cuts on her face and chest and came away red and sticky. She would never again be the pretty little blonde girl from Rockville. Gerri felt the terrible violation of her body. She lay trembling as waves of pain passed through her. Tears ran freely down her face. Her future was forever changed. Time seemed to stand still until her screams brought the attention of a passerby. Police and paramedics soon arrived and rendered aid. Hospitalization, stitches, rape kits, interviews, embarrassment, and regret became her life and the end of a family vacation.

Gerri would have her day in court. She would testify before a room full of strangers and live through the entire ordeal again. She would see the monster that had ravaged her sent away. Though scarred for life, Gerri would eventually go to college, graduate, and move far from Maryland where she had seen her childhood innocence taken away in a single night. Her nightmares and dark memories would remain her burden to carry.

3

FRIENDSHIP

Lonnie was tried and convicted of rape and assault with intent to kill. Due to the seriousness of his crimes he had been waived from juvenile to adult court. On the Eastern Shore of Maryland, the judges were still law and order types who didn't hesitate to dispense real justice, especially when the crime was well published and the reputation of the family resort was called into question. Better for the town to rid themselves of this predator.

Lonnie's mother didn't have the resources to hire a high dollar attorney so Lonnie was left in the hands of a young public defender who did his best, but was no match for a seasoned prosecutor and a fourteen-year-old girl whose face still bore the scars of the savage attack. The jury took very little time to return a verdict and the judge had no problem in sending Lonnie away for twenty years for his crime. With good behavior he would not be eligible for parole for at least ten.

When he entered the Maryland penitentiary, he was small and weak. That made him easy prey for the hardcore inmates who ran the institution even more so than the correctional officers. Sex offenders seldom find sympathy from guards or inmates, no matter where they are incarcerated.

He quickly became an easy target for the aggressive bullies and a few brutal prison guards. Rape is an ugly crime and even inmates have sisters and girlfriends. They could easily imagine them at the hands of this demented punk. Repeatedly being raped and beaten by fellow inmates became a norm for Lonnie. He had never cried as a kid on the street, but he cried almost every night now.

After a futile attempt by Lonnie to defend himself, he quickly learned that he should align with someone who could protect him and keep the animals at bay. Lonnie became the "Bitch" for Donavan, a guy who lived by his fists and his reputation. Donavan was 6'3" and solid muscle. He was not gay, but prison brings on certain needs and a new fish named Lonnie filled those needs. Lonnie's life became one humiliating experience after another as he was openly used as Donavan's sex toy, serving at the pleasure of his protector. Nearly every night Donavan would demand a blow job or bend Lonnie over the lower bunk and ream his ass. It was still better than being a punching bag and a pass-around for an entire cellblock.

For seven years Lonnie remained protected. His protector spent a great deal of his time working out with weights and punching a heavy bag that hung in the exercise yard. Lonnie began lifting small weights and hitting the bag, but it barely moved with the power of his punches. Over time, Lonnie began to see changes to his own body. He gained about thirty-five pounds of lean muscle. He learned the art of protecting himself. No one would screw with him now, but he still remained with the man who kept him safe.

When Lonnie's protector was released from jail, Lonnie

was housed with a new inmate named Billy Ray Snelling. Billy Ray was serving ten years for several armed robberies that he had been tied to in the Salisbury, Maryland, area. Billy Ray was 31 years old and Lonnie learned quickly that Billy Ray was pretty worldly, as he told Lonnie of some of his experiences and places he'd been. Although Lonnie refused to admit it, he had grown to tolerate, if not like, the company of a male sex partner. Billy Ray saw it as a mutual benefit and they became close friends as well as lovers. In this relationship there was both give and take by willing partners.

During the last three years of Lonnie's stay in prison, a great deal of time was spent talking to Billy Ray about his life and how he had ended up in jail. Billy Ray told Lonnie that he lived alone with his mother and needed to help her with the bills and expenses. Billy Ray said this is why he had begun robbing people. It never came up as to why Billy Ray had never sought honest employment.

Billy Ray said he had pulled far more robberies than were known to authorities. They linked him to several through fingerprints and DNA, which neither he nor Lonnie fully understood. During the telling of these stories Billy Ray described how he had used the threat of a very large knife to frighten most of his victims into giving up their money and possessions without any resistance.

Billy Ray called the knife a KA-BAR and said he had gotten it when he was in the Marine Corps. He said he first saw one when he went to Parris Island, South Carolina, for boot camp. He said the knife had a 7" blade and a 5" leather-wrapped handle. A knife that's a foot long gets everybody's attention. He explained that during boot camp he had been shown how to use this Marine fighting knife by a crazy-fuck of a drill instructor. Billy Ray said this guy would pull this black-bladed knife from its sheath and make the recruits try and take it away from him. He said they were armed with hard rubber knives and told they could stab the instructor during the training. Billy Ray said this guy used to kick the piss out of everybody, never got stabbed and forcibly took their rubber knives away from them. Then he would do some kind of karate shit throwing them to the ground and then menacing them with his real knife. The training was brutal, but Billy Ray said he learned how to use it to the level expected by the Marine Corps. He had been taught to use the KA-BAR as a killing tool.

Billy Ray had some minor trouble with the law when he was younger. He chose to go in the Marine Corps as a way of straightening himself out. Of course, eight months after boot camp, his Marine Corps experience ended quickly when he took a swing at a non-commissioned officer who promptly broke Billy Ray's jaw and helped him get a bad conduct discharge. Billy Ray said he was very proficient with the KA-BAR, but had never killed anybody. He said the Marine Corps had taken his away at the time of his discharge, but he had stolen one from a fellow Marine before being kicked off the base.

Lonnie, skeptical but fascinated by this story, had Billy Ray teach him the moves he learned in the Marine Corps. They used toilet paper rolls taped together as their KA-BAR. The training was fun for Lonnie and he started to feel the power such a weapon might bring him. After all, it was the three-inch knife he used on Gerri that had been his downfall. During court testimony, the doctor who had worked to save her life said the short-bladed knife had failed to penetrate deep enough to cause fatal wounds. It was only the lack of length in the blade that had saved her, and doomed him to years behind bars.

As their friendship grew, Billy Ray revealed that the police never recovered over eight thousand dollars in cash and some valuable jewelry he had stolen during his most successful robbery. This was actually a home invasion, where Billy Ray had worn a mask and gloves. The mask and gloves saved him from the police linking him to that particular incident. The KA-BAR also remained among the missing evidence. Billy Ray laughed and said the police had walked all over it, but never found the hidey-hole in the floor in his bedroom. He said one leg of his bed stood on the piece of wood that concealed his stash. When he got out he planned to use it to jump-start his new life.

Lonnie knew he was the one who would get out first, and armed with this information, the stash would jump start his new life rather than Billy Ray's. After all, what are friends for if they can't help you out? Billy Ray's mom might be a problem, but he would deal with her when the time came. Might even give Lonnie a chance to test his new knife skills.

Marine Corps training provided by Billy Ray continued. Lonnie learned how to set ambushes and cover his tracks so enemy forces wouldn't detect him. Billy Ray was a great teacher and loved seeing Lonnie absorb the training like a sponge. Billy Ray would probably have made a great Marine if he weren't such an asshole.

Three years after being assigned Billy Ray as a cellmate Lonnie left jail, feeling he could easily be a member of the Marine Corps if that was something he wanted to do. Ex-cons are not welcome in the Marine Corps, so the thought never crossed his mind again.

4

FREE AT LAST

It was November, 2020. Ten years was almost up and Lonnie was eligible to be released from prison, having earned credits for good behavior. Release was scheduled for early December. Before leaving jail, Lonnie had been ordered to report to his parole officer in Salisbury within twenty-four hours of his release. It was here that ground rules for being a parolee would be laid out.

Lonnie's mother had dealt Lonnie her final act of abandonment by dying two years after he went to jail. He had been escorted to her funeral by armed correctional officers, but remained handcuffed the entire time. It would have been embarrassing but for the fact there was no one else in attendance. She had been buried in a pauper's grave on the outskirts of Sandpiper. Another lost soul committed to the ground to await a second coming or reincarnation or just the bugs that scratched at her cheap coffin shortly after it was covered by damp, dark soil.

Because of his mother's death, Lonnie had no one to sponsor him for a release on parole. Billy Ray had talked his own mother into allowing Lonnie to use their address so that he could be released from jail. Billy Ray had also talked a cousin into giving Lonnie a job working in an auto body shop. With a residence and a job, the release went smoothly. Both Lonnie and Billy Ray knew that Lonnie would neither live with his mother, nor work for his cousin. Lonnie had made it clear to Billy Ray that after reporting to his parole officer he would be in the wind. No more rules for Lonnie. Ten years had been enough. Lonnie vowed to never return to jail or be under anybody's thumb ever again. Lonnie told Billy Ray he needed to set some things straight, but would then be headed for California for a new beginning.

On Friday morning, December 7th, Lonnie kept his appointment with the parole officer and said all the right things and promised to be good. He was sure all new parolees said the same thing.

While Lonnie was still in Salisbury, he paid a visit to Billy Ray's mother. He charmed her into believing his visit was to thank her for her kindness in giving him an address to use on this parole application and to assure her that Billy Ray was doing fine and would be home himself soon. Lonnie had learned from Billy Ray that the only bathroom in the house was upstairs. Feigning his need for a toilet, Lonnie went upstairs and quickly slipped into Billy Ray's room, quietly moving the bed a foot or two and removed the floorboard concealing the stash. To his delight, the treasure was housed in a green canvas bag with the markings USMC stenciled on its side in yellow. A quick look revealed the money, the sparkle of jewelry, and the KA-BAR still in its leather sheath. The sheath also bore the Marine Corps initials. The bag was small enough for Lonnie to hide it under his coat for the few minutes he remained to say goodbye to Billy Ray's mom. The entire thing had gone much smoother than he expected. He hadn't had to resort to hurting the old lady to get what he wanted. It was a win-win all around, except for Billy Ray who wouldn't know he had been screwed for at least another two years. Lonnie thought, *guess that will end our friendship. Fuck him!*

5

BECKY'S PLACE

It was Friday, December 7th, when Lonnie left Salisbury and hitched a ride to Sandpiper. He made sure the Marine Corps bag was prominently displayed, which he was sure would help him catch a ride. It was Pearl Harbor Day. Who wouldn't help a Marine on Pearl Harbor Day?

When Lonnie arrived in Sandpiper he went to the District Court to see if any of the people who had sent him away were still around. Revenge against one or more of them would be sweet before he left town. Lonnie showed up at the District Court around 1:00 p.m. Knowing they would have metal detectors, he stashed the Marine Bag containing the KA-BAR and jewelry behind a dumpster about two blocks away; the cash he kept in his jacket pocket.

Lonnie entered the court and passed through security without notice. He kept his head down so as not to look into any surveillance cameras that would surely be guarding the lobby and halls of the court. None of the old retired cops working the entrance had been around when he was last there. If they had been, it was doubtful they would recognize him in his new buffed up body and with ten years of aging to his face.

He went to the very courtroom where they had decided there was enough evidence to bring him to trial. This was the first step in destroying his life. Lonnie would never consider that it was he who had ruined his own life and that of a young girl on vacation.

Lonnie sat near the back and watched the proceedings, a series of minor criminal cases. None of the court officials looked familiar. Lonnie was looking for the judge and one particular woman who he would love to kill if she was there. The woman was probably retired or dead by now because she was in her late fifties when he had sat at the defense table in the front of the room. He didn't remember her name, but he would never forget the look on her face as she would place evidence on a table before the bench for the judge to see. No one else saw it, but Lonnie saw the smirk on her face. He knew she was laughing at him and thinking how stupid he must be to not even be able to commit murder against a defenseless girl of fourteen. Lonnie was right because no one else did see the woman laugh at him. Her kind and forgiving smile turned to laughter only in the eyes and mind of the demented killer sitting at the defense table.

Lonnie observed a young girl now performing the same duties. The judge, different from the one who had sent him away, called her Peggy and she responded like a puppet to his every command. At one point, Peggy left the courtroom and had to pass right by Lonnie. He couldn't believe it—she laughed at him. It was almost exactly the same smirk he remembered from so many years ago. He knew she was thinking—*Loser*. In that fleeting moment, the dye was cast. He would visit ten years of hate and rage on the bitch named "Peggy." Now he just needed to figure out how he would do it.

Lonnie hung around until 4:30, the normal closing time for the Court. He went outside and retrieved his Marine Corps bag and positioned himself where he could watch the door by which all the employees left. At first, they came out in a surge, and then in a trickle, and then no one. Had he missed her? At 4:40 she came out by herself. She had changed her clothes and was now wearing light blue sweat pants and a matching sweatshirt with a hoodie. She crossed Ocean Highway and walked the two blocks to the Boardwalk. She crossed the Boardwalk and went to the water's edge where she turned left and began jogging north. Lonnie paralleled her, staying on the Boardwalk. At 13th Street he was forced to move to the beach and follow her by jogging in the sand near the water. There were dozens of people walking and jogging the beach so he went unnoticed by Peggy and everyone else. It was obvious that Peggy did this frequently because she actually appeared to pick up the pace and was still going strong at 25th Street. Lonnie had done a lot of weight lifting and bag punching, but seldom ran in the exercise yard. He now found himself winded. He stopped and crossed the beach back to Ocean Highway. He started walking south towards the Courthouse. Lonnie realized this might take a little more planning and perhaps setting an ambush or trap, but with his newly learned Marine Corps skills, he didn't doubt his ability to get it done.

When he reached 18th Street and Ocean Highway, he saw a bar called Nickels and Dimes. The sign announcing cold beer was all it took to make him deviate from his journey. He hadn't gotten shitfaced in years and Billy Ray's money was burning a hole in pocket.

A few drinks would help him think through his problems. Booze and drugs had worked when he was seventeen; surely it would work now.

When Lonnie entered the bar, it was about half full and he chose a bar stool near the entrance where he could observe the comings and goings of the folks. The bar filled up quickly and the volume of the crowd almost made him feel like he was back in his cellblock where the noise never stopped.

Around 8:00, the entrance door opened and a girl stepped through; she was alone. She looked around, and it seemed she was looking for a seat rather than people she knew. The only seat at the bar was next to Lonnie. She approached and asked him if it was taken. He smiled, said no, and invited her to have a seat.

She sat down and checked out the Marine Corps bag sitting on the foot rail at Lonnie's feet. He had purposely positioned it so the yellow USMC was clearly visible. It was working its wonder as several people had noticed it and responded by nodding their approval. One guy even bought him a beer and departed for his table with a "Semper Fi." Lonnie hadn't learned what that meant, but returned the gesture by raising his bottle in a salute.

The girl now sitting next to Lonnie had medium length dark hair, almost black, and dark eyes to match. She had a cute smile and straight white teeth. She was a little overweight and dressed a little frumpy for the beach. Most would have thought her pretty, but she thought of herself as fat. She lacked self-confidence. She had no rings on her fingers and appeared to be a little out of her element, sitting alone at the bar.

Lonnie moved quickly to make her feel relaxed by asking

her if she was waiting for friends. He told her there was already a short wait for tables once you gave the waitress your name. She sheepishly said, "No, I'm alone tonight, but I wanted to get a drink before calling it a night."

Lonnie came back quickly saying, "I'm alone too." He told her he had just return from a tour of duty in Afghanistan. The Marine bag carried the day and she seemed impressed. He said, "You look nice and it's great to have someone to talk to. I've kind of lost my social skills being in Afghanistan and away from girls for the most part. I feel lucky the only empty stool was next to me. Would it be alright if I bought you a drink?" His current build and haircut was also consistent with his story. Had she been a little sharper she would have noticed his pasty white skin was more in keeping with a just released inmate than a veteran coming back from a desert assignment.

Two lonely people soon found equal ground. She shared information about her family, friends, work, likes, and dislikes. Her name was Becky Marshall. She lived in Harrisburg, Pennsylvania, and worked in the office of a small travel agency. Becky admitted she was not really a travel agent, but handled most of the paperwork associated with booking cruises and vacations. She was confident she would be a full-fledged agent soon. Becky was twenty-three and single. After a couple of drinks provided by Lonnie, Becky admitted she had a boyfriend. They had a fight and she came to the beach to get away from him and get some time to think about her future with him. Becky's parents were retired and had moved to Oregon after vacationing in Sandpiper a year ago. She had no siblings.

Becky told Lonnie she had her own apartment in Harrisburg, but her boyfriend was pushing her to let him move in so they could share expenses.

Every time Becky tried to obtain personal information about Lonnie he would say he had grown up in the area. He told her both his parents were dead. He said his most recent memories were about death and dying in Afghanistan and were not a good topic for conversation. Becky said she understood and appeared to be drawn to this lonely Marine just home from the war.

The bar was busy with people coming and going. There was a lot of laughter and clinking of drink glasses. A live band was set up in a far corner playing country music. The crowd seemed to like them by the clapping and cheering at the end of each song. During short band breaks the juke box would kick right in, filling the bar with music. Some couples were dancing on a very small dance floor. The place was alive and the smell of beer filled the air. The lights were dimmed. Alcohol and dim lights made everybody look good. Great place to be on a December night.

Becky was clearly not a heavy drinker. She began to slur her words and giggle at the slightest bit of humor. Lonnie began to think this was a golden opportunity presenting itself and asked her where she was staying. She said, "I'm staying in a condo right on the beach that belongs to an acquaintance. It's within walking distance, but my car is in the bar parking lot." Lonnie suggested they have one more drink and then he would see that she got home safe. She thanked him and went off to visit the ladies room. While she was gone Lonnie grew anxious to get her alone. He was sure he could convince her that her boyfriend was probably fucking someone else tonight so she should use her temporary freedom to explore her own options.

Becky's gait was a little unsteady when she returned from

the restroom. She gathered her purse and coat to leave. Lonnie would not let her pay any part of the tab and tipped heavily to impress her. He grabbed his bag and walked out the door with Becky. Once at Becky's car, he convinced her she was in no shape to drive and if she would trust him, he would drive her the short distance to her condo. She agreed and tossed him the keys. Lonnie hadn't driven in over ten years so he was very careful and deliberate. Becky was too drunk to notice his lack of skill behind the wheel.

She directed him to the condo that turned out to be right on the beach on 21st Street as she said. The condo was facing the beach where Peggy had jogged just a few hours before.

Lonnie parked the car where she directed and noticed that this first-floor condo was one of six units joined in a row. Becky's car was now the only car on the lot. When he remarked about the lack of other cars, Becky said that people who own them seldom used them in the winter. She said it was likely no one else would be around the entire weekend.

Lonnie walked Becky to the door and put his hands on her shoulders and turned her towards him. He bent his head to kiss her and she moved into him and kissed him full on the lips. No words were spoken, as Becky opened the condo door and left it ajar as a signal for him to come in behind her.

The KA-BAR in the Marine Corps bag came into the condo with Lonnie. It appeared both had found a new home at "Becky's Place."

6

THE WEEKEND

Lonnie was very pleased with himself. Becky turned out to be a willing and anxious lover. The alcohol had loosened her morals and her thinking. The argument with her boyfriend and finding a Marine hero had caused her to put all caution aside and fully engage in a long night of lovemaking.

Lonnie found that Becky was more than willing and able to meet his sexual hunger. The long stay in jail and his maturity had enabled him to rise to the occasion over and over again throughout the night. A far cry from the young kid who ejaculated at just the thought of having sex. They had found two unopened bottles of wine and continued to fuel the drunken stupor that enhanced their lovemaking, even if it was only in their own minds. Lonnie asked Becky to try things that she had never done before, but she repeatedly rejected all advances beyond missionary position sex.

It was obvious to Becky that Lonnie was disappointed. He aggressively pushed for her to cross into new territory with him. Even alcohol couldn't persuade her to do the things he was suggesting. She was enjoying getting even with her boyfriend, but knew this was a weekend fling that would probably end in the morning. She was on the pill, which gave her protection. Lonnie refused to consider using a condom. Becky's lack of self-confidence led her to believe that when the Afghanistan veteran awoke he would take one look at her chubby body and grab his shit and go.

Lonnie and Becky shared a mutual release of intimate urges. There was a lot of foreplay, as each explored the other's body, with touch, and kisses. Becky was meeting his every thrust with her legs wrapped around him and her heels digging into his ass. The sex was good for both of them and they soon succumbed to fatigue and fell asleep.

The sun was well above the rolling ocean before Lonnie stirred and questioned his own whereabouts. It all came back when he saw the nude female asleep next to him. He assessed her with sober eyes and knew she wasn't a ten, but she wasn't a three either. She was certainly better than his bed partners over the last ten years. He thought about what they had shared and was pissed at her. He had not been able to talk her into some stuff he thought would be more satisfying had she tried it. He was very fond of oral and anal sex and she had rejected both. Even doggie style was beyond her repertoire.

His mind shifted to the condo and the opportunity it offered him to complete his task of taking care of Peggy. He left the bedroom and gazed out the window at the beach only a few steps away. He wasn't sure how he could lure Peggy into the condo, but he was sure if she got this close, he would figure it out.

In the meantime, a piece of ass was nothing to scoff at and he had one waiting for him. He returned to the bedroom and nudged the sleeping girl awake. She looked surprised to see him and actually thanked him for staying with her. Maybe she thought he would screw her and just leave. He probably would have had it not been for the prime location of the condo.

Because they were both still naked, Lonnie rolled on top of her and took her again. Her breath was nasty this morning from the drinking the night before, but he figured his breath might be a little funky too. She eagerly took him inside her with unrestrained enthusiasm.

When they were done they decided they needed to take a shower, and nothing gets you going like a slick wet body, so they did it again standing in the shower. He tried to go down on her, but she pushed him away and made him stand up. They almost knocked the side out of the glass shower, but eventually did get cleaned up.

They dried and dressed for the day. Lonnie said, "I really appreciate you and enjoyed last night." She was starved for love and attention and responded, "So did I, Lonnie. You were so sweet and I'm glad you were here with me this morning. I think we found something that both of us have been missing. Do you have plans for today?" Lonnie suggested they get something to eat and then decide what they wanted to do. They were very hungry and drove to a nearby restaurant where they ate a full breakfast. Lonnie again paid for everything. Hell, it wasn't his money so why not. He saw Becky had quite a bit of money in her purse and figured he would eventually get that money too.

They returned to the condo and spent most of the day having sex and watching movies on the television. Becky said she was having a good time and wished she didn't have to leave on Sunday and go back to work. Lonnie continued to suggest more adventurous sex. Becky rejected every suggestion, which began to raise Lonnie's level of frustration.

Lonnie had bought several more bottles of wine and a thirty-pack of Budweiser, which meant they could hole up for a couple of days. Whenever they got hungry, they used Becky's cell phone to call for carryout pizza and subs. Lonnie paid cash and tipped heavily, continuing to impress Becky.

Lonnie knew he had to come up with a plan. Sunday was coming fast and he didn't want Becky leaving with a story about a guy she had shacked up with near the scene of a murder that was about to occur. Before he knew where this would lead he had made the mistake of telling her his real name. He had made a mistake in his effort to remove Gerri as a witness. She had lived to tell what he had done. Prison taught you that witnesses and physical evidence were a certain way to end up back in the slammer.

Becky said she wanted some chips and dips, and would run out to get them. Lonnie agreed, and while she was gone he explored the condo more thoroughly. He discovered a locked owner's closet. The KA-BAR made quick work of the locked door. Paperwork in the closet revealed the owner to be Scott and Patti Nolan. Lonnie found it full of toilet paper and other supplies the owners would not want to tote every time they came to the beach. The owners also would not want it consumed by anyone renting the place. One plastic box contained first aid supplies, a bottle of sleeping pills, gauze, and surgical tape. He found maintenance stuff, including hammers and screwdrivers. He also found the tool that fixes everything—duct tape.

A plan quickly formed in his mind and he closed the closet door after taking the sleeping pills and the hammer into the kitchen. He dumped the pills into a folded dishcloth. He pounded the dishcloth until the pills were pulverized into a powder, then dumped the powder into a small paper cup and placed the cup on the top shelf of a cabinet above Becky's reach and eye level. He returned the hammer to the closet and washed out the remaining powder in the dishcloth and hung it over the spigot of the kitchen sink.

When Becky returned, Lonnie used his practiced lying and charm to keep her happy and totally off guard. They ate, drank, watched TV, and had sex on the couch, floor, and coffee table in front of the TV. Life was good!

Becky kept saying she was so sorry she would have to leave the next day and asked Lonnie where he would go when they left the condo. He told her he had some Marine buddies in the Baltimore area and would try and hook up with them until he could find a job and get his own place. Becky gave Lonnie her cell phone number and made him promise to call her once he was established. She told him Baltimore wasn't that far from where she lived and maybe she could slip down and visit with him. He agreed, knowing full well this would never happen.

Around 10:30 p.m., Lonnie started serving the wine to Becky. It was now laced with the sleeping powder from the top shelf. He introduced it in small amounts so as to not change the taste of the wine. Becky wanted to fully enjoy her last night at the beach so she drank freely. Around midnight she felt the overwhelming desire to close her eyes. She fought the urge and kept on drinking. Lonnie made love to her and she quickly drifted off into a deep and unrelenting sleep. Lonnie carried her to the bedroom. She was already undressed so he just laid her on the bed. He then went to the owner's closet and retrieved the hammer, the screwdriver, and the duct tape.

Becky didn't even stir as he began to tape her wrists and ankles to the headboard and footboard of the bed. The hunger was building inside of him. She would no longer deny him and his sexual appetite would soon be sated. He ripped about a ten-inch piece of tape and stuck it to a corner of the nightstand. Next to it he laid the hammer, the screwdriver, and the KA-BAR. Lonnie retrieved Becky's cell phone and removed the battery from it. He stripped out of his clothes and lay down next to her. He quickly fell asleep. Sunday morning was fast approaching. The end of a perfect weekend would soon be at hand. Becky slept unaware.

7
BECKY IS IN TROUBLE

Becky's eyes snapped open. She stared at the popcorn ceiling above her, trying to clear her head. She had been hung over before, but this was different. She was groggy and confused. She was weak, so weak, she couldn't move her arms or her legs. It felt like they were very heavy and she just couldn't lift them. She turned her head and thought perhaps she was still asleep and having a bad dream. Her gaze followed her arm to her wrist. It looked like it was encircled with silver tape. She turned her head the other way and saw the other wrist looked the same. Lonnie was there and he looked normal. He had no tape on his wrists. She raised her head and looked down the length of her body and realized for the first time she was nude, not even covered by a sheet. Her legs were spread at an obscene angle that she immediately tried to correct, but her legs would not move together and she saw why. The same silver tape encircled each ankle. The tape went out of sight over the edge of the bed where the footboard was located. How had this happened? Had she been so drunk last night that she had allowed Lonnie to bind her to the bed while they were having sex? She knew Lonnie would suggest something like that, but it would be something she would never agree to. Or would she?

Lonnie slept on like nothing was wrong. It must be something she agreed to before falling asleep. She pulled hard at the tape on her wrists to see if she could break loose, but she didn't have the strength or the leverage to make it happen. Her legs were also bound in such a way she could not release herself. She would have to wake Lonnie and have him remove the tape. It was so embarrassing to be seen in this position in the full light of day. So vulnerable to be seen like this, but she had no choice.

Becky whispered, "Lonnie wake up. Lonnie wake up." His eyes opened slowly and he turned his head and met her wide eyes. "Lonnie, what happened last night? Help me get out of these tapes."

Lonnie did not speak, but rose from the bed and moved to the footboard and looked down upon her. She again tried to close her legs, but it was hopeless. "Please Lonnie, this is embarrassing me. Undo the tape please."

Lonnie had the most evil smile on his face that she had ever seen on a human being. He was naked, and instead of moving to help her, he began stroking himself to a full erection. He moved over the footboard and hovered over her before entering her in one quick and cruel movement.

It hurt and she let out a whimper. She told him to stop. This wasn't funny and he needed to stop. Rather than stop he increased his tempo and reached a climax within seconds. He withdrew and moved to the side of the bed near Becky's head. By this time tears were streaking down her face and she was struggling to get out of her bonds. Lonnie reached to the nightstand beside the bed and for the first time she saw the hammer, screwdriver, and a very large knife.

Lonnie picked up the knife and held it close to Becky's face. He said, "Becky, listen to me because I will only tell you this one time. I don't want to hurt you, but I will. If you scream I will tape your mouth and I will cut you bad." To emphasize his words, he laid the knife on the side of her face so the tip was very close to her eye.

"I am not who you think I am and I have something I must do before I leave here. You will stay with me until I finish my business and then I will turn you free to go home. If you fuck with me I will kill you and leave your body here to rot. I have killed people before so I will not hesitate. If you understand and agree to behave yourself just nod your head."

Becky quickly nodded her head and asked Lonnie what he had to do and why he had to tie her up. Lonnie laughed and said, "If I tell you then I'll have to kill you. Do you still want to know?" Becky became quiet as tears continued to flow.

She was in a confused state of mind, but realized she had made a terrible mistake by letting this stranger into her life and into her bed. Fear of what was to come raged in her brain. *Stay calm. Do not resist. Survive.*

Lonnie said, "While I wait to do what I have to do we can party together. I'll show you some stuff that will make you a better lover for the next man you're with. Your boyfriend will be thanking me for the education I'm about to give you. Please don't resist me. The slightest scream will make me cut you to death. Do you understand?" Becky nodded her head. She understood.

School started almost immediately as Lonnie taught Becky about oral sex. The slightest resistance on Becky's part was met with the tip of the knife cutting her inside her legs close to her vagina. These cuts were very small, almost like paper cuts, but they stung and she tried to cooperate. When she became passive during the sex acts he would prod her with the tip of the screwdriver or threaten to rape her with the handle of the hammer.

The hammer had a very long handle covered in some type of rubber. There was no doubt the damage the introduction of this instrument into Becky's body would cause. She gagged and almost choked when he held her head to his crotch and had an orgasm. The entire time the knife was held where Becky could see it and she knew the slightest wrong move or sign of reluctance could result in being cut. "Becky, it's not all about me." He went down on her and performed cunnilingus. He was so rough that if there was any pleasure to be found in the act, it was lost.

Becky thought Lonnie was letting her loose when he maneuvered her by releasing the tape on one wrist and then one ankle. Before she could figure out what he was doing he had placed her face into the pillow and mounted her from behind. She felt wetness between the cheeks of her buttock and smelled a sweet odor that reminded her of the pancakes they had had the previous day for breakfast.

Lonnie was using an old jailhouse trick he had learned early in his incarceration. Syrup was an excellent lubricant if used quickly before it became too sticky. The pillow muffled her scream as he plunged into her rectum. He told her she would come to enjoy this kind of sex. He had done so in jail.

At one point she begged to be allowed to go to the bathroom. He turned this into a humiliating experience by wrapping his belt around her neck like a leash and leading her into the bathroom. Standing at the door he watched her relieve herself.

He forced her to drink a full glass of wine, telling her that she needed to stay hydrated. The wine was laced with the sleeping powder that he now used in a much larger dosage to knock her out. He finally tired of her and retaped her to the bed. He threw a sheet over her body— his only act of kindness all day.

Before she fell asleep, Lonnie told her he had to go out and since he couldn't trust her to be quiet, he would be taping her mouth. He told her he would stand outside the condo and if he heard her making noise he would come back in and cut her throat. He took a ten-inch piece of duct tape and placed it across her mouth. The sleeping powder was already having an effect and she did not resist. Thirty minutes later she was sound asleep. While she slept, Lonnie went to a nearby pharmacy and obtained additional over-the-counter sleeping pills to keep her malleable and quiet. When she awoke again it would be Monday and Lonnie would begin his sex lessons again.

Monday came. Becky's will had broken easily. She allowed him to do whatever he wanted to her body. She even went to the bathroom with him watching without protesting. Every orifice of her body had been violated. She was racked with pain; her body was no longer her own.

The small cuts he had inflicted hurt like hell, but so far he had not damaged her beyond healing. Her plan at this point was to do whatever he wanted and hope that when he completed his business he would just leave her. She had no doubt she had fallen into the hands of a very angry psychopath who would kill her without hesitation or remorse. Staying alive would require complete submission—and a whole lot of luck.

Around 1:00 p.m. on Monday, Lonnie decided he needed to go to the District Court. He would check on Peggy and work on his plan to extract revenge from her for laughing at him. He thought he might drag her into the condo and let her join his sex school. That would be difficult in the daylight. He would have to wait for an opportunity and then act.

He made sure that Becky was well drugged and taped her mouth again, telling her any effort to escape would result in a very slow and painful death. She fell into an almost coma-like sleep before he even went out the door.

Lonnie took Becky's cell phone and her car to the District Court. He parked down the street because he didn't want to park on the court lot. He left his Marine Corps bag and KA-BAR locked in the trunk of the car and entered the court. Keeping his head down and averted from the surveillance cameras, he returned to the same courtroom and watched an almost instant replay of Friday's activities. Different defendants were there, but the same old excuses were being presented and the same old lawyers were asking the court to forgive their clients for all their wrong doings. The fix was always in. Defendants got PBJ and were ordered to pay the court costs. The Court got its money.

The lawyer would then walk out in the hall and receive the thanks of the client who had mistakenly thought he was going to jail. The defendant would then turn over his hard-earned money to the lawyer for his representation. The lawyer got his money. The criminal justice system in action. It didn't work for Lonnie. He didn't get probation—he got fucked, but he was back to make it right.

Lonnie saw Peggy moving around the courtroom, smiling and bowing to every wish of the judge. It was sickening and so was she. He never made eye contact with her, but he was sure that she was looking at him. When he wasn't looking she was laughing at him, even if no one else could see it or hear it. Damn her soul to hell.

He got up and left the building. He moved Becky's car to a position where he could watch the employees leave the court. Just like Friday, Peggy came out prepared for her run. Today she wore a pink hoodie and sweat pants. Wasn't that special! She probably had a different color for each day.

Lonnie knew what would happen next so he drove all the way to 14th Street, parked the car, and entered the beach. He stood by the water and waited. Soon he saw her coming toward him. He was about five or six blocks from the condo. He would follow her and then close the distance between them when they got to the condo. If he had a chance and no one was watching, he would come up behind her and possibly hit her in the back of the head and render her unconscious or senseless. He would then pretend to come to her aid and remove her from the beach to the condo.

She passed by him without seeming to notice him. Lonnie heard her screaming, "Loser". He fell in behind her and covered ten blocks quickly. He recognized Becky's condo building as he drew close. Lonnie was astounded to see four people near the water directly in front of the condo building. A man and three children were surf fishing. Could he pull it off with them so close? He closed to within about fifteen yards of Peggy. He placed his hand on the KA-BAR hidden beneath his jacket. He intended to use the handle to inflict a blunt force strike to the back of her head. Lonnie was going to do it. Now was the time.

Lonnie's luck ran out with a scream. Not from Peggy, but from one of the children surf fishing. "Pop-Pop, I've got a bite. It's a big one I can tell."

Peggy swerved to the right and ran up beside the kids. Lonnie could hear her encouraging the child to pull hard and bring the fish in. Pop-Pop was now by her side and Lonnie was standing there like a fool. He turned and jogged up towards the condo building. He would return for the car later. Becky would pay for his disappointment. Tomorrow he would come up with a better plan. Why was life always torturing him?

8
A DAY OF PAYBACK

Monday night had not been good for Becky. Lonnie unleashed all his frustration on her. He hurt her simply for the joy of hurting her. The sex was so rough and so degrading that she had run out of tears. The bed smelled horrible because of the body fluids, sticky syrup, spilled beer and wine. Becky had not been allowed to bathe since their shower together so she was now producing her own odor that, rather than deter Lonnie, seemed to heighten his interest in her.

On Tuesday morning, Lonnie spent a great deal of time in the kitchen and left Becky alone, for which she was grateful. She called to him only once when she needed to use the bathroom so badly she couldn't wait any longer. He took his sweet time coming and she had leaked urine onto the bed, adding to the repulsive odors.

Around 3:30 in the afternoon, he taped Becky's mouth and warned her to be quiet. He said he may be able to complete his business today and would then allow her to leave. He started to cover her with a sheet, but had second thoughts and left her fully exposed. He squeezed her breasts for luck and said he would be back in a few hours and that he might even bring a female friend to join in the party. Becky shuddered at the thought of some other poor girl being lured to the condo. She closed her eyes and prayed this nightmare would end soon.

Lonnie was ready at 4:30 when the employees burst from the courthouse. He had already done his advance work and knew Peggy was working today, but she was late leaving. As the minutes ticked by, Lonnie became more and more concerned that he had somehow missed her or that she had used some other exit to leave the building. He knew the office area of the courthouse where Peggy worked. As daylight began to dwindle he saw the office lights in this area remained on. He needed to stay patient and focused. His hand lay on the Marine bag on the seat next to him. The power of the knife seemed to emanate from the bag. Today was the day.

At 5:00 the employee door opened and Peggy emerged in a dark colored running outfit. She was really late today, but that would work in Lonnie's favor as daylight was turning to darkness. He worried she would shorten her run and his plan would be thwarted again. She crossed the street and headed for the beach.

Lonnie swung into action and drove quickly all the way back to Becky's condo. He then ran back about ten blocks and entered the beach. He was surprised to find it empty of other people. He knew he was ahead of Peggy and jogged north, back toward the condo. When he reached 18th Street he removed his jacket and smoothed away his footprints. He then turned into the deeper softer sand of the beach. Lonnie cupped his hands and furrowed out a trench about the length of his body. The sand was soft. It only took a couple of minutes to accomplish this task. He lay down in the trench with his head facing the ocean. He used his arms in a reverse snow angel, sweeping sand over himself as best he could. Billy Ray had taught him about ambushes and camouflage. Be a part of the environment is what he had been told. Lonnie was now a part of the beach. He waited.

He could hear her before he saw her. Her shoes slapping on the wet sand announced her coming. Lonnie had found gloves in the owner's closet and now wore them. He had the KA-BAR in his gloved hand and was prepared to rise up and rush forward, knocking Peggy to the sand and taking control of her.

When she reached his location she suddenly stopped and was looking at the sand before her and behind her. She slowly turned toward the ocean and appeared to be looking at the breaking waves. Lonnie saw his chance and rose slowly from the sand like something out of an old horror movie. He moved close to Peggy and sensed her turning toward him. He reached his gloved hand to cover her mouth.

He had her. She was not like Becky. Her body felt like it was made of steel. There was no fat, only lean muscle, which was beginning to tense as realization was taking hold. Lonnie's plan to take her back to the condo evaporated as he realized she would be too strong and too quick for him to manhandle across the beach. Maybe if he stuck her a little with the knife she would give up.

To the contrary, when the knife entered Peggy's body, it set off all the alarms handed down to humans since the beginning of time. She began to thrash in an effort to break free.

He plunged the knife to the hilt. Lonnie remembered Billy Ray instructing him to wiggle it around for maximum damage. It worked. The fight left Peggy almost immediately and the weight of her body pulled them both down on the beach. He whispered in her ear, "Who's laughing now?" Peggy said nothing because she was dead. Lonnie then withdrew the KA-BAR.

He thought about what a trophy this girl would have been in the bedroom of the condo, but now he just needed to get away. He darted across the soft sand until he got to the buildings on the other side of the dunes. He stayed in the dark shadows of the buildings and looked to see if anyone was around. Coming down the street carrying a bucket and a fishing rod was an old man. Had he seen Lonnie? He didn't think so because he never even glanced towards Lonnie's hiding place. The old man passed through the dunes in the direction of where Peggy laid. Lonnie wished he had put her in the water. Maybe the tide would have taken her out. No time to worry about that now. Time to get back to the condo. He was pumped. Adrenaline was surging through his body and he felt no remorse. He felt alive for the first time in years. Payback was sweet; so sweet he might have to take another day or two in Sandpiper. Only Becky knew he was in town and she wasn't going to be telling anybody.

While he was thinking these things, he was unconsciously stroking the blade of the KA-BAR. It was still wet with Peggy's blood. He knew he should feel remorse for what he had done. Instead he felt elation over fulfilling his dreams. He knew this was twisted and evil thinking, but his soul was black and he thirsted to bring more suffering to the people he perceived had wronged him.

9
BROGAN

At 6:20 p.m. the phone rang incessantly, as it always did in the offices of the Sandpiper Police Department. The call was answered by Bonnie, a police communications officer and then quickly routed to the detective bureau. Detective William Brogan promptly answered it. Nobody ever called him William, and only strangers called him detective. Everyone who knew him just called him Brogan.

Brogan is forty-four years old, but has the looks of someone still in his early thirties. Brogan, a twelve-year veteran of the Sandpiper Police Department, has been a detective for all twelve of those years. He came from the Baltimore City Police Department where he had been a homicide detective. His career was cut short in Baltimore City when he arrested one of the city councilman's son for a particularly gruesome murder of a working girl. The subsequent scandal and news coverage almost unseated the city councilman, and the mayor himself when he tried to use his influence to get the boy off on a lesser charge. Brogan never did play well with others, especially those in positions of power. He refused to play along with a lesser charge. His testimony was the key to the prosecution's case. The subsequent conviction saw that justice was meted out on behalf of the victim and her family.

The prosecutor was pleased and began to position himself for his own rise in the political ranks. The chief of police on the other hand served at the pleasure of the mayor. The chief soon got his marching orders to make a manpower reduction of one — Brogan got the message. He could have fought his removal, but he knew his life at Baltimore PD was over. Instead he found a home in a less demanding and less corrupt environment. Sandpiper, a Maryland seaside police department.

The town fathers of Sandpiper were only too glad to have a trained detective join their ranks. The city attorney vetted their applicant and learned his dismissal was politically motivated. The mayor and chief never even considered making him serve as a patrol officer. They recognized the value added to the department by hiring a man of his caliber. The rank and file were at first jealous and angry over the "new guy" coming in and taking a sought-after detective position without serving his time on the street.

Brogan suffered a dramatic reduction is salary, but he was single and had few needs. His love of police work allowed him to ignore a lot of the creature comforts that others sought in a profession. A local ocean city businessman was only too happy to provide very affordable housing within the city limits. Even though it was an investment property, the very pro-police businessman decided he would rather have a cop living there. Two bedrooms and a short walk to the beach made Brogan feel like he was on vacation year-round. He loved the town and town began to love him back.

Brogan proved his worth quickly by demonstrating his leadership abilities and innate investigative skills. He showed appropriate respect and regard for the uniform officers in the department. He worked with them to clear minor criminal cases, but left the credit for a successful closure with them. He quickly learned the names of each officer and their family situations. He did ride-a-longs with every shift, listening closely to their perceptions of what was right and wrong with the department. He offered suggestions to resolve situations and suggested they offer solutions rather than complaints. Most of the officers were much younger and less experienced than Brogan, and began to trust his judgement and advice.

Patty Ryan and Bob Carr were the other detectives working for Sandpiper PD when Brogan arrived. At first there was some resentment, but that dissolved as they realized they would personally benefit from the lessons Brogan would give them in policing. Especially doing so as a detective. He told them as Sandpiper grew so would the detective bureau of the police department. He convinced them that they were favorably positioned to grow and move upward in the ranks. He accompanied them at crime scenes and during interviews. He maintained a position as team member rather than someone giving tasks for others to do. Again, successful closures and accolades were left with his detectives. The chief loved his management style and saw the harmony growing within his ranks. Some officers remained aloof and suspicious, but slowly, they too were joining the Brogan team.

Brogan was a "presence" wherever he goes. He was 6'2" and weighs 210. His thick dark hair had just enough silver to give him a roguish appearance. His steely blue eyes would look right through you. Those eyes made him very attractive to the opposite sex and he didn't shy away from this advantage. He would have made a good politician with his naturally good looks and quick smile. Fortunately, Brogan did not have the other qualities of a politician. He didn't lie, steal, or negotiate. Brogan was black and white with no middle ground. Known to bend the rules to the breaking point if it meant he could take a bad guy off the street, he was a no bullshit kind of guy. He had been involved in the martial arts and worked out his entire adult life. It often served him well in his role as a police officer. Many potential fights and confrontations had ended quickly when he used learned techniques to render his opponents crying for mercy while showing no marks or visible injuries. So far, all these situations had been "resolved" in Brogan's favor.

Married and divorced when he was younger, Brogan was no stranger to women and love—as long as it only lasted for a night or a weekend. In a beach town like Sandpiper, there were many opportunities for these types of relationships. It fit well with his lifestyle as a cop. When he was working a case, he would often go for days with little sleep, little to eat, and no time to be explaining himself to some woman who demanded his attention. They all said they understood his job, but they never did until he showed them. He was able to flourish in this atmosphere of no commitment.

Brogan answered his phone the same way every time. "Brogan!" The caller was a young temporary summer police employee who had hung around after the other temporary officers returned to college or other endeavors at the end of the summer. Officer Quincy was talking too fast and too loudly to be understood. Brogan told him to slow down and lower his voice. Quincy slowed a fraction and switched to a whisper that made him even harder to understand. Brogan heard the words "body on the beach at 18th Street." This was enough for Brogan to lean in closer to his phone and begin to scratch notes in the notebook he always carried inside his jacket pocket. The date, the time, 18th Street, body, and Quincy's name became the heading.

Sandpiper's jurisdiction covers approximately eight miles of Maryland's ocean front property. Once a small and quiet village, it was now dominated by hotels, high-rise condominiums, nightclubs, and tourist-oriented businesses. There were also your mandatory amusement rides and arcades where the kids could spend their parents' money at record speed and be rewarded with a stuffed animal or a plastic toy. The growth of the city was quickly being matched by the growth of the crime rate. While violent crime was rare to almost non-existent, things like theft, assault, public drunkenness, and burglary surged like the ocean surf with the summer crowds. Along with the young people came the drugs. During the summer days the beaches were crowded with half-naked people who then retreated to the darkened bars and clubs at night. "It's always fun until someone gets hurt – then it's hilarious!" Those who had moved to the hilarious stage often occupied the detention cells at the PD.

Winter was different. This was December and the city catered to an older, more mature acting crowd of people. A body on the beach was suspicious merely by it being there. Nobody is swimming or lying on the beach this time of the year. Drug overdoses were normally confined to hotel rooms or parked cars where it was warm.

Brogan knew better than to ask this young officer to give his opinion as to what happened. Brogan's orders were quick and concise. "Secure the crime scene. Don't let anyone near the body and get identification and record the names of anybody who may be a witness."

Brogan checked with the police communications officer and learned there had been no radio transmissions concerning this situation. He was grateful for that little bit of good news. It would give him a head start on the ever-present media and the normal, Lookie Loos who always showed up at crime scenes just to see what's happening. He told the PCO to keep radio silence and to alert detectives Ryan and Carr via cell phone that he was in route to a "body on the beach at 18th Street."

Brogan grabbed his overcoat and headed towards his police car. His gun was secured in his shoulder holster; his flashlight was in his car. He would wait to make any further needed notifications once he had a chance to check the scene. The time was 6:30 p.m. Tuesday, December 11th. Hell, of a time to be dead.

10
THE DISCOVERY

S andpiper's Police Department is housed in the center of town, on Ocean Highway. It only took Brogan seven minutes to arrive at 18th street and the beach. He arrived at 6:37 p.m. He saw Officer Quincy's vehicle parked at the opening in the dunes. These openings permit people to walk onto the beach. The dunes act as protection and buffer between the ocean and the buildings along Ocean Highway. This also creates a visual barrier for those at street level. To see what is occurring at water's edge you must enter the beach or be in one of the elevated rooms of a hotel or condo.

Quincy's car was turned off and dark. There was no sign of the him. This was good because it probably meant that Quincy had stationed himself somewhere on the beach near the body.

Before proceeding onto the beach, Brogan donned surgical gloves to prevent contaminating any evidence that may be present. He also took note that there were no other vehicles parked close to this particular location. How had the deceased arrived at the beach? Brogan was thinking victim, but until cause of death was determined it was an unattended death. Brogan scanned the area looking for potential witnesses, cameras, suspects, or things that may hinder or help with his impending investigation. He saw nothing helpful or unusual. With flashlight in hand, Brogan made his way between the dunes and onto the beach. The dim light of another flashlight directed his movements slightly to the left after passing through the opening in the dunes. He walked towards the flashlight and closer to the surf.

Quincy stood like a centurion guarding the scene. Unfortunately, there was not much of a scene. The dark shape of a body lay on the beach in the wet sand just out of reach of the water. The tide was going out and it was clear that at one point the water had probably reached the body and beyond. The sand was smooth and slick with no signs of footprints or struggle. There were no drag marks in the sand. It was like the body had been dropped from the sky. Keeping a good distance from the body, Brogan went directly to Quincy and asked him what had happened.

Quincy said he was proceeding north on Ocean Highway when an older gentleman at the intersection of 18th Street waved him down. Quincy referred to his own notebook and said the man's name is Jerry Johnson and he lives at 13278 18th Street, Bayside, Sandpiper, MD. His phone number is 410-555-3436. Quincy was telling Brogan what would eventually appear in his report. He was attempting to show the detective he had been thorough and competent in the handling of the scene.

Quincy reported that Johnson is seventy-one years old and surf fishes nearly every day after it gets dark. Johnson had told him the fish bite better after dark. Johnson's residence is a short walk across Ocean Highway and straight out onto the beach between the dunes. He said he carries his bait, pliers, extra hooks, rod holder, and a rag in a five-gallon bucket in one hand and his surf rod in his other hand. Once on the beach he empties the bucket of its contents, turns it over, and uses it as his seat.

Johnson told Quincy that he had followed his routine, but that when he got near the water's edge he had noticed a dark form on the beach. He said he first thought it was a large piece of driftwood or perhaps a large dead fish that had been washed ashore. Curious, he had moved to the dark form and finally realized it was a person lying on the beach. He thought some drunk had wandered onto the beach and passed out. It was way too cold and the person was lying way too close to the water to be left there. He decided he would try to arouse the person and send them packing. Johnson said he set his bucket and rod down and went over to speak to or shake the person and get them up and moving.

When the person lying on the beach failed to respond to his voice commands to wake up, he gently nudged the person. He said he touched the neck of the person, to see if there was a pulse, but he found none, and the skin was cold and damp. He realized that the person on the beach was probably dead.

Johnson said he left his rod and bucket on the beach and moved as quickly as he could back to Ocean Highway to seek help. He was on his way home to call the police when saw a marked patrol car driving on Ocean Highway and waved it down. When Quincy stopped, Johnson told him what he had found and led the officer back to the body. Quincy questioned Johnson about seeing anyone else on the beach or near the dunes. Johnson said he had seen no one and heard nothing.

Quincy said he examined the bucket of fishing equipment and patted the old man down for safety, confirming his identification via his driver's and fishing licenses.

Quincy saw that Johnson was beginning to show some effects of his discovery and the chill of the ocean air. The combination of the two was creating small tremors in the old guy's body. Quincy told him to take his bucket and his rod and go home. He told him not to discuss his observations with anyone and that a detective would be contacting him soon to conduct a more thorough interview. It appeared to Quincy that Johnson was grateful to be getting off the beach and left immediately. It was then that Quincy called the police department and asked for the detective unit.

Quincy reported to Brogan that he had personally checked the body for a pulse and signs of life, but finding none, touched nothing else. He said he believed the deceased to be female and white.

After hearing Quincy's report, it was clear how quickly the crime scene had deteriorated. The killer, Johnson, and Quincy had all stood next to the body and yet their footprints had already been swept away.

Brogan was facing a scene that would surrender little in the way of leads. He could only hope the body would reveal evidence leading to the cause of death. It was still way too early to determine that this was a crime. Brogan would treat it as a homicide until irrefutable evidence said it was not.

11

A GATHERING

Brogan pulled his cell phone from his hip and speed dialed the chief of police. Chief Ellwood Richards answered on the second ring. Caller ID told the chief it was Brogan calling—and Brogan never called unless it was important.

Brogan quickly filled the chief in on the scant information that was available. Brogan told him, "I'm only calling you because you never know when the media may be tipped to the crime now under investigation." The chief didn't like to be surprised and neither did the mayor. He appreciated the call and asked no questions. He knew Brogan would update him when he had more information. Chief Richards would be reaching out to the mayor the instant this call ended.

Brogan's next call was to the local medical examiner, Doctor Michelle Vickery, whom also took the call before it could go to voice mail. She answered the call with a single word, "Vickery."

"Hi Doc, this is Brogan. We've got a body on the beach at 18th Street. No visible wounds, but other than checking for a pulse we're not sure what we got. Nobody has come forward yet to say they saw anything. I'm treating it as a homicide until you or the evidence tells me something else."

Vickery responded, "I'm about 10 minutes away. Get me the crime scene guy and hold what you have."

Brogan said, "You got it. See you in a few."

Brogan had history with Michelle. They had a brief romantic interlude, after working several crime scenes, shortly after he had been hired. She had been on the rebound from a marriage gone south, and he was a shoulder to lean on. Brogan suspected the relationship was an effort to get even with her cheating husband, but Brogan was okay with that. She wasn't the first woman he had provided with safe harbor and a place to lay her head. Protect and serve is the motto. She's a good person, but like Brogan, she's always working, and the brief encounter died on the vine. They parted friends, remained friends, and never mentioned what had happened between them.

Vickery was a local doctor, who doubled as a medical examiner. Her practice was based in Salisbury. She knew her legal limitations, and would quickly send a body to the state medical examiner's office if the circumstances were suspicious or if homicide is determined. Dr. Vickery would make this judgment call based on what she found at the crime scene. She always came to the crime scene. She once told Brogan, "I cannot determine what has happened by looking at a body in the sterile setting of a hospital or funeral home." She has one other local doctor who would cover for her during vacations or periods of personal illness. So far, she had never been too ill or too busy to go to a scene. Tonight was no exception.

No sooner had Brogan terminated this call he became aware of three people moving toward him from the dune line.

All were carrying flashlights and he recognized the outline of two of them as being detectives Patty Ryan and Bob Carr. The third person was Sloan McCoy, crime scene investigator for the Sandpiper PD. McCoy carried a box full of evidence collection material. Brogan knew that as soon as McCoy saw the situation he would also be bringing his spotlights and cameras to the beach, so he could complete his task of evidence collection. Brogan also knew that either Ryan or Carr had anticipated the need and notified McCoy. McCoy was very thorough and had helped to make many cases for the PD. He would need all of his skills at this scene because it appeared it would offer little to help them find the reason this body was here. If this was a murder, McCoy's findings might be the key to identifying the killer.

Brogan made one more call to Nelson Horn. Nelson worked as the on-call duty driver for the Barringer's Funeral Home. There had been a long-time arrangement between the PD and Barringer's. Because it was the only funeral home within the city limits they had agreed to come to any crime scene or unattended death to remove the body unless relatives made a specific request for another funeral home. In this case, there would be no one to make a request this evening. The funeral home had also agreed to transport bodies to Baltimore if so directed by Vickery. This agreement had worked well over the years and Horn said he would be in route in approximately twenty minutes. He would stand by at the scene as long as necessary to transport the body. Horn, from prior history, also knew not to discuss this new assignment with anyone else prior to coming to the scene. Even the funeral director, Mr. Barringer, would not learn of this pick up until the next morning.

All the players had one thing in common: they all mistrusted the media and knew that once they became involved all bets were off as far as keeping anything secret. The killer would know everything the media did. In this small city the rumor mill would be rampant with both good and bad information. It would be a "clusterfuck."

Brogan also had a personal reason for keeping the media on the back burner for as long as possible: his hit and run love life had one exception—and that was Lynn Murphy who covered the police beat for the local, but wildly popular, TV station, Channel 7. She was particularly popular because she was drop-dead gorgeous and still available. She and Brogan had met shortly after he came to work for the PD. He had used all his best moves to lure her into his bed with the intention of moving on after adding one more notch to his belt. Their professional differences were a wall that would always stand between them. Her need to know and his stance on keeping everything secret had no possible resolution. He often wondered if he had really lured her or if she had used her charms to disarm him and leave him vulnerable.

Regardless, they were not exclusive, and continued to seek each other out for comfort and companionship when either felt extreme stress in their life. This happened about every six months. Once they went for fourteen months without seeing each other. They both agreed during their first meeting that it would serve neither of their careers any good if their relationship became known. When the itch happened, they would travel to a discreet and distant hotel to meet. This was a secret both had promised to keep and so far, both had kept the promise. Brogan hated this chink in his armor and didn't need the distraction in an investigation he suspected was going to demand his full attention.

Brogan, Carr, Ryan, and McCoy tossed about theories as to how the body had come to be found on the beach. They examined the areas away from the body to see if anything looked out of place. They all agreed to wait the short period of time it would take for Vickery to arrive before approaching the body again. Brogan felt it best to use a team approach from the very beginning. He listened to what they had to say and weighed it in his mind. While waiting, Brogan said, "Carr and Ryan. Start canvassing nearby condos, hotels, and businesses for additional witnesses once Vickery has examined the body. Go check each building for any security cameras pointed toward this area of the beach." He knew darkness would be their enemy, but every possibility needed to be pursued. "Check all the bars within normal walking distance. Give them special attention to see if there were any disturbances or domestic altercations." The investigation would move more quickly if they could make an early identification of the victim. Brogan gave Ryan the name and address of Jerry Johnson and instructed Patty to interview him tonight in the hopes he remembered something that might be significant. Each time Brogan made an assignment, all three detectives would make an entry in their notebooks so that nothing would be forgotten and their reports would follow a chronological order. Detectives Carr and Ryan were always learning and improving their basis of knowledge. They would not go home until ordered to do so. They were good cops and getting better. Brogan had brought big city procedures to Sandpiper. If this is a murder, by tomorrow there would be a Murder Book growing with entries of every detail of this investigation. All interviews, statements, lab reports, photographs, and relevant information would find its way into this book. The Murder

Book would be the one place where investigators now and, in the future, could go to and find everything that occurred and had been done during the investigation. It was organized in chronological order and sectioned off for special reports such as the medical examiner's report and lab reports. Photographs would be in the book with extensive notes about what each photograph depicted, who took the photograph, and where it was taken including date and time. Detectives assigned to the case would pour over this book time and time again looking for something they may have missed or for a lead that was never completely resolved. The Murder Book would grow from a large binder to multiple binders depending how long the case lasted. Should it become a cold case, new detectives would be assigned to review and update the Murder Book every year. Generally, murder cases are never closed unless they are cleared by an arrest.

Vickery was escorted onto the beach by Quincy who was now stationed at the dune entry to prevent civilian interference and to continue to gather identification of anyone who came too close or showed an interest in what was going on behind the dunes. "The criminal always returns to the scene of the crime" was still in vogue and not to be ignored, even in these days of sophisticated criminals. Many a bad guy is now in jail because he just couldn't stay away after he had done his dirty deed.

Vickery acknowledged all the detectives with a nod of her head and a comment. "Hi everyone, let's see what we have." She joined with McCoy and the rest of the detectives as they moved next to the body. Brogan and the other detectives also moved in close behind them. Vickery formally declared the body was deceased. Brogan made a note of the time. McCoy had already photographed the body from what seemed every possible angle without touching it and now brought his camera to bear for closeup photos. Vickery told McCoy, "Sloan get a picture from this angle. Get a closeup shot looking from the water and then go around and get it from the dune side. I'm going to pull the hood back so take several pictures of the face when it's revealed." Vickery gently pulled the hoodie far enough back to reveal the victim's face. There was a very low gasp from all those bending in close to the body as they simultaneously recognized the victim as Peggy Williams, an employee of the District Court. Not only was she a local, she belonged to the exclusive club known as the criminal justice system. Williams was a very young and healthy woman. Her lying dead on the beach screamed crime of violence. Solving this crime was going to be a top priority for all those gathered there tonight. Chief Richards, Mayor Stanley Wells, and Administrative Judge George Nelson would soon be putting pressure on Brogan and his people to clear this case quickly. This was going to be a very personal case to the entire community.

Vickery made a cursory examination of the body and found what appeared to be a large stab wound in her side. Vickery ordered Williams removed from the beach, and transported to the Baltimore City medical examiner's office for a full autopsy by Nelson Horn who had been standing by with Quincy at the dune line. Vickery supervised the body, left fully dressed, being gently lifted on to a clean white sheet laid next to her on the beach. Hopefully any hair or fiber transfer from the suspect would be captured should it be dislodged from her clothing during transport. Brogan, Carr, Ryan, and McCoy all assisted in lifting the sheet containing the body into a plastic body bag that was then zipped closed. The body bag was then placed on a funeral cart and carried from the beach to the awaiting Hearse.

12
THE NOTIFICATION

The update call to Chief Richards had not gone well. The chief knew this victim and instantly realized this would be a major problem for him and his police department if it was not solved quickly. He told Brogan to use every resource available and to call him if he needed anything. Overtime was authorized. A briefing for the mayor and administrative judge might be wise, but Chief Richards said he would get back to Brogan in the morning on whether that would take place. Detective Ryan had learned that Peggy Williams lived with her parents, Jack and Martha, on Sharon Avenue in Sandpiper.

Brogan cut the other investigators loose to begin their interviews and neighborhood canvasses while Vickery and McCoy finished up at the scene. Vickery had no hesitation about her decision to send this body to the state medical examiner's office for a full autopsy. Hopefully it would produce some shred of evidence to lead them to the killer, because the scene wasn't giving up anything.

Vickery pulled Brogan aside and said, "It's clear to me that Peggy has been stabbed with what appears to be a rather large knife. There is only one visible stab wound which might be unusual except the entrance wound was so large that if the length of the blade corresponded with its width, multiple stabs were probably unnecessary. There were no visible defensive wounds and at first glance there appeared to be no skin or blood under her fingernails. Whatever happened had happened fast and probably right where the body lay." Nevertheless, her hands were bagged to protect against the loss of any evidence. Body temperature was obtained, but would be of limited value in determining time of death due to the fact she had been exposed to the cold beach, and even colder ocean water.

Brogan called the shift sergeant at the PD and ordered the beginning and continued patrol of Sandpiper's beaches. It was doubtful this would produce anything, but not doing it would be a disaster if something else happened on the beach.

Brogan wondered, *where had Peggy been and why did she end up here?* Tracing the hours and her movements prior to her death may lead to its cause.

Brogan had told the chief he would make notification to the parents. After the body had been removed for transport to Baltimore, he went directly to the Williams' residence.

When he arrived, he found a typical Sandpiper beach home with the required amount of nautical decorations including brightly painted clay fish and a small lighthouse, sitting in a bed of seashells, adorning the front yard. A small front porch with a couple of rocking chairs. The porchlight on. The lights inside gave the house a warm and welcoming feel. This was absolutely the worst part of being a cop. No matter how many times Brogan had done this it never got any easier.

He knocked on the door and a small, white dog came charging around the corner of the hall and bounced off the front door with a noisy greeting. Moments later a woman, probably in her mid-to-late- sixties, came down the same hall and peered out the glass of the front door. She recognized Brogan from his many appearances in the District Court, which had been her workplace for nearly thirty years. She had retired to join her husband, Jack, who was already retired. The best thing that happened at the time of her retirement was her daughter Peggy, recently graduated from high school and looking for a job had taken her place. Martha Williams had no doubt her long service had influenced the selection, but she hoped it was because they were seeking the same strong and loyal work ethic she had given the court all those many years. Peggy was cut from the same cloth and was soon earning her own accolades from those she worked with daily. Chief Judge Nelson was especially fond of Peggy and treated her like a daughter. He had a daughter the same age.

There was no fear or concern in Martha's eyes as she opened the door to the tall, good-looking Detective. There had been no personal contact with him in the court, but Martha often heard some of the younger women swooning over this single man who carried a gun. She would chuckle to herself over some of the goofy plans these girls would come up with to trap this guy. They never executed the plans and of course none of them ever trapped him. He obviously kept his personal life and his professional life separate.

It was the serious look on Brogan's face that gave Martha her first moment of pause after she opened the door. She stepped back to allow him to enter the entrance hall. The little, white dog sniffed madly at Brogan's cuffs and then lost interest and moved away. "We need to talk," Brogan said, "Is your husband home?"

Jack Williams had heard this exchange and centered himself in the hallway behind his wife. They both showed curiosity, but not really concern. Without comment, they led Brogan into their small kitchen. As they went down the hall, Brogan saw several pictures of a much younger Peggy engaged in different sports activities including basketball, softball, and track as well as other school events. One picture showed her with a boy about her same age. Both were smiling and standing closer than just friends. Was this a boyfriend, perhaps?

The house was very neat and tidy. It had all the delicious aromas that come from cooking a homemade dinner. The kitchen table was set for three, but no food had yet been placed upon it.

Brogan waited until all were seated. "I'm sorry. I have some really bad news and there is no easy way to tell you." Martha and Jack sat close, but could not grasp what may have happened.

"It's Peggy. She was on the beach today and was attacked." Martha stood straight up as if her chair had catapulted her into that position. "Is she alright? Where is she?"

Brogan knew that beating around the bush only made things worse, so he came straight out with it. "Peggy was stabbed during the attack and died as a result of her wound. She has been removed from the beach by the medical examiner and will be taken to Baltimore City for autopsy. This is a murder investigation. I personally assure you that I will do everything in my power to find the person responsible and bring them to justice. I'm very sorry for your loss."

No sounds came from Martha or Jack. Tears streamed

down Martha's face and Jack just stared straight through Brogan who sat uncomfortably wanting to begin questioning them, but waiting for this information to sink in.

Brogan asked them if he could call anyone for them or if there were anyone else they would like him to contact. They shook their heads in the negative, but then Jack said, "Does Jimmy know?" Brogan asked, "Who is Jimmy?" Jack said Jimmy Aiello is Peggy's boyfriend and he is away at college at the University of Maryland in College Park. Brogan obtained a phone number and an address at the college for Jimmy and promised to have someone make face-to-face contact as soon as possible. Brogan made a mental note to get that done quickly and have College Park PD try and establish if Jimmy had an alibi for the time frame of Peggy's murder. Brogan made a written note in his book recording the time of notification of next of kin and recording the name of Jimmy Aiello. He wished he could be there when Jimmy was notified. Much is learned in the first moments of someone learning of the death of a relative, friend, or lover. People who commit murder seldom know how they should react when they receive the news.

Brogan asked the parents if they were up to answering some questions to assist him in his investigation. Both were still visibly shaken, but agreed to try and help as much as they could. Brogan learned that Peggy and Jimmy were planning to get married when Jimmy graduated from college. They liked Jimmy and told Brogan that he had dated Peggy all through high school and treated her like gold. He came back home nearly every weekend and they were inseparable. They obviously had no reason to suspect him of any act of violence against their daughter.

They told Brogan that Peggy was extremely happy with her job at the court and would recount the many cases she heard on a daily basis. She especially liked to talk about the funny cases that came before the court and the way Judge Nelson seemed to be able to resolve them so everybody left feeling like they had won something. Judge Nelson could be stern and didn't hesitate to send a jerk to jail, but would often soften in the following days and shorten the sentence of the defendant that by then had learned his lesson. Peggy never mentioned having any problems at work.

Peggy was very health conscious and never varied from her regiment of running on the beach after work. She would change clothes at the court and then run for five miles. Two and a half miles one-way and then turn around and run back to the courthouse where her car was parked. She shared her daily activities with her mom and boasted of her dedication to staying in shape by her daily run. Brogan made a note to check the car for potential evidence. He wondered if Peggy's routine had been a contributing factor to her death. Bad people have a way of taking advantage of good people's routines.

The parents had held it together longer than most, but now they were beginning to fall apart as reality set in. Peggy was their only child, and she was never coming home; their life was ending without them actually dying. From this point forward, they would live in the past and find little joy in the days to come. They would put on a good face and say that Peggy's death would not be forgotten and that during her short time on earth she had contributed to those around her. It was all bullshit. She was gone and she took their dreams with her.

As Brogan left the Williams' house, Martha told him that she didn't know what she would do with Pistol, Peggy's dog.

He would wait near the door every night for her to come home. The dog looked up at Brogan as he went out the door and then lay down to await his owner. *Sorry Pup,* Brogan whispered to himself, as he stepped from the porch, *Your life is also forever changed.* Brogan knew he had to find this asshole even if it would never make everything right again. Someone had destroyed this family and Brogan would not rest until he evened the score. He would find justice for Peggy.

13
MEDICAL EXAMINER'S OFFICE

It was Wednesday, December 12th. The sun was not up yet, as Brogan crossed the westbound lanes of the Chesapeake Bay Bridge. While most people were still sleeping Brogan was fully awake, alert, and anxious to discover any evidence that would help him solve this murder.

One advantage of having been a Baltimore City homicide detective was the connections he had with the state medical examiner's office located in Baltimore. For years, there had always been a Baltimore City police detective assigned to work in the medical examiner's office. The detective acted as coordinator and liaison with all police agencies in Maryland. A longtime friend of Brogan currently held that position. Sergeant Charlie Connolly had been put on alert and was awaiting Brogan's arrival.

Connolly is a thirty-five-year veteran of the Baltimore City PD. He was a very large Black man with a gruff voice and a toothy smile that seemed to have been permanently implanted on his face. He had been a homicide detective for about ten years before being assigned to the medical examiner's office.

On the rare occasion that a murder or suspicious death occurred in Sandpiper Beach, the autopsy would miraculously end up as the first autopsy performed the following day, due to Brogan's friendship with Connolly. Helping the dead speak starts very early in Baltimore. Bodies arrive from all over the state throughout the night. They are greeted by staff that logs them in with all available information. This information is passed on to the doctors who perform the autopsies. The medical examiner's medical staff begins this gruesome task at 7:00 a.m. seven days a week.

Brogan was always present for his autopsies. He knew the best information and evidence was gathered firsthand by being present to observe and ask the questions necessary to move the investigation in the right direction.

If Brogan had his way he would personally conduct every interview, every search, and every step of the process. He was smart enough to know that time was his enemy during a death investigation. He needed the help of other investigators. During his time with Sandpiper PD he had helped hone the skills of his fellow investigators and was now comfortable that they all worked off the same sheet of music.

Those who investigate death learn quickly that the dead have no voice other than the one provided by those who explore their demise. There is no greater responsibility for a homicide detective.

As was Brogan's practice, he pulled into the parking lot at the medical examiner's office at 6:00 a.m. He always arrived early. He was admitted via a back door used only for personnel of the office and police officers. He went directly to Connolly's office and found his longtime friend sorting through reports piled haphazardly on his desk.

"What's going on Charlie?" Brogan asked.

Charlie looked up and then at his watch. "Should have known it was you. Always want to be the first guy through the door. I skipped breakfast this morning just to be here ahead of you."

Brogan responded with a broad smile. As Charlie rounded his desk to embrace Brogan in a manly hug he said, "Don't tell me I look like I haven't missed any meals, and by the way my wife says hi and thank you for allowing her to sleep in this morning."

Charlie looked Brogan up and down and said, "How do you stay in such good shape Brogan?"

"Working out and chasing women." Brogan responded giving Charlie a big smile of his own.

Peggy's body had arrived during the wee hours of the morning and was currently stored in a refrigerated unit with a sliding drawer. A toe tag was placed on her body providing the date of her death, her name, the county where her body came from, and the police agency charged with investigating her death. She was dressed just as she had been found on the beach, minus her shoes and socks that were sitting next to her feet.

"What are we working on this morning?" Charlie asked. Brogan explained that the victim in this case was an employee of the District Court. Brogan told Charlie, "I think this may be an attack on the criminal justice system, but it was far too early to confirm that theory." He shared the little information he had with the sergeant. Connolly agreed saying "Whoever the killer is, we need to take them off the street." The two seasoned police officers continued their friendly banter as they walked the short distance to autopsy suite. As it always did, their mood shifted at the double door. This was a place where professional behavior was the rule. Respect for the deceased and concern for all those impacted by this death fell squarely on the shoulders of this team.

At 7:00 a.m. Brogan stood very close to the autopsy table in a brightly lit area. The stainless-steel table was slanted slightly to allow blood and bodily fluids to flow into a drain tube at one end of the table. There was a hard rubber wedge device at the high end of the table where the deceased's head is placed to elevate it off the table. This autopsy area, was similar to a surgical suite in a hospital with knives and saws gleaming and ready for use. There was a microphone strategically placed over the table so the doctors could record what they are doing and what they were finding during their examination.

Two morgue technicians, clad in hospital-type scrubs, brought Peggy's body into the examination suite. Peggy had been removed from the body bag, but was still wrapped in the sheet that she had been placed on at the beach. They gently lifted her body from a rolling cart onto the autopsy table.

While under the scrutiny of Sergeant Connolly and Brogan, the men slowly undressed Peggy's body, taking each item separately and gently placing it in separate evidence bags for further microscopic examination at a forensic lab. The lab would be looking for trace evidence to help identify the perpetrator. A single hair, a flake of skin, or a drop of bodily fluid could turn a case. With the wide use of DNA, any of these items could provide all the evidence needed to put a suspect and a victim together. The technicians photographed each article of clothing, wrote down date, time, description and other pertinent information that would be used to track the evidence to its final storage location and maintain a chain of custody. They were particularly careful in removing the clothing covering the upper portion of her the body because these items contained the cut made by the knife or sharp instrument used to end her life. The cut in her clothing would be measured, evaluated, and preserved as evidence. Finally, the sheet was carefully folded and placed in a separate bag for further microscopic examination.

When this process was complete, Peggy lay nude. Brogan saw that she had been very fit from her running and exercise, and aside from the large gash in her side, it looked like she could sit up and start talking. While her undamaged skin was flawlessly smooth, the coloring was wrong because the blood had settled to the bottom portion of the body. When her heart stopped pumping, the blood in her body reacted to gravity and sought its lowest level.

Peggy was fully photographed, then measured and weighed using scales built right into the autopsy table. By now one of the medical examiners assigned to do the autopsy was standing by to begin his examination. Dr. Theodore Ramsey supervised as one of the technicians, known as a diener, stepped forward and cut the body open. The flesh was pulled back and a rotating saw was used to cut the ribs and remove the breastplate from the victim, exposing all Peggy's organs. Ramsey then stepped forward and began his examination. During this entire process no one spoke. Only the doctor would speak, describing what he was doing and what he saw during his examination. The only exception would be questions the doctor may have of the attending police officer. The doctor, upon completing his examination, determines the cause of death and renders a professional opinion on the nature of the death. Generally, a death is classified as natural causes such as disease or heart attack or accidental death, suicide, or homicide. In rare cases it can be classified as undetermined.

The examination lasted approximately an hour and it became clear early on that an otherwise healthy young female had died as the result of a single penetration wound, most likely caused by a large knife. The entry point and organs were examined very closely along with the track of the blade. It was determined that once the knife had been inserted it had been moved around without being extracted until after death had occurred. There was some bruising to Peggy's lips and mouth area that was interpreted as having been caused by someone clamping their hand over her mouth to keep her from screaming. The lack of other fatal wounds led the doctor to conclude that Peggy had most likely died quickly as a result of the massive damage to multiple internal organs caused by the knife.

The knife wound was carefully measured. The depth, breadth, and size of the hilt were all recorded. These measurements were close, but not exact because the knife had been moved around during the attack.

During the autopsy, Peggy's heart, liver, lungs, and brain were removed from her body and placed before the doctor. He dissected each organ looking for possible disease or other evidence that may explain her death. These organs would be further tested, along with blood, urine, stomach contents, vaginal, anal, and mouth swabs.

When the autopsy was complete and the sound recording equipment had been turned off, Dr. Ramsey, Brogan, and Sergeant Connolly spoke about the findings. Ramsey said, "I suspect the weapon used is a large hunting knife or similar weapon, perhaps a military style combat knife." The blade had ridden along a rib and left a faint residue. Ramsey stated, "The direction of the wound strongly suggests the perpetrator is right-handed. The moving of the blade once inserted and the lack of repeated strikes may indicate someone with experience or prior training with a knife. Stabbing cases frequently involve multiple stab wounds reflecting the passion and anger of the assailant."

The doctor had removed a small portion of Peggy's rib and would have it examined independently. During the autopsy and the conversation that followed, Brogan made notes on everything that was done and said. A very detailed autopsy report would follow, but that could be a week or more coming. Ramsey said, "I'm sorry I can't talk with you longer, but as you can see the room is filling up and I must move on to the next case. After you receive my report, please call me if you have any questions or concerns. If any of the test results show something out of the ordinary I will call you immediately to help you with your ongoing investigation."

With no immediate questions from Brogan and thanking the doctor, both he and Charlie left the suite and returned to Charlie's office. They attempted to catch up on everything that was going on in Baltimore City and the up-tick in homicides across the state. Charlie's phone was ringing off the hook. More dead bodies were coming, and police officers were looking to Charlie for help.

As Brogan left, he told Charlie, "If you ever get a day off, why don't you come on down to the beach and I'll set up a day of fishing on one of the local charter boats? I've made friends with some of the captains, so it probably won't cost us anything and if it does I'll pay. We go ten miles out in the Atlantic and you'll finally get away from the phones. It'll be fun. Give me a call and I'll do the rest."

Charlie responded enthusiastically, "Yeah, I'd like that. I'll call you soon as it gets warmer." Charlie was a big city boy, so Brogan doubted that call would ever come.

Disappointed because the autopsy had revealed very little about the killer, Brogan began the trek back to Sandpiper. He called Detective Carr and told him, "The murder weapon is most likely a large knife. Maybe a hunting knife or a military style combat knife. Share this information with Ryan and McCoy and no one else."

While a very slim lead, he asked that all of them keep the description of the knife in mind, when conducting interviews. Unfortunately, the Eastern Shore of Maryland is a hunter's paradise and hunting knives are abundant. There is no shortage of patriots on the Shore, so military style knives are also plentiful. Still it was something and little things could never be ignored. Breaks in a case came from strange places. A bit of luck and a lot of good police work were usually the key to solving these types of cases.

Brogan thought back to the stabbing cases he had handled in Sandpiper and realized that there had actually been very few where there had been intent to kill someone. Upon his return to the PD he would conduct a computer search to identify prior stabbing cases and determine if there could be a connection. Stabbing someone was very close and personal and few people had the nerve to pull it off. Guns were usually fired at a distance and allowed the perpetrator some margin of safety while still rendering the victim dead.

Detective Carr told Brogan that the initial neighborhood

interviews had revealed no additional witnesses or pertinent information. The search of Peggy's car had been completed and nothing was found that might point to her attacker. The car had been fingerprinted and the results of those fingerprint comparisons were still pending. The car had been found locked and there were no signs of violence in or around the car. Hotel and condo surveillance cameras were not focused on the beach area where the body was found, but one camera had taped a single male subject coming off the beach and standing near a building while an old man with a fishing rod entered the beach nearby. Due to the darkness and lack of lights on the building the identification of the subject was doubtful unless a suspect was developed by other means.

Detective Carr conveyed he and Detective Ryan had interviewed the administrative judge and learned that he had asked Peggy to remain past her normal departure time to complete some needed tasks that had taken about an hour. The judge said that nothing unusual had happened and Peggy appeared to be her normal happy self when she left. Carr said the judge was very upset about this situation and was blaming himself for holding Peggy over to help him. The judge said he had been aware of Peggy's habit of jogging the beach, but assumed she would forgo it due to the late hour leaving the court.

Carr said to Brogan, "Me and Ryan spent a great portion of last night reviewing the courthouse surveillance tapes. We found an anomaly that we can't explain. We discovered on the Friday, Monday, and Tuesday tapes of the same white male entering the courthouse and then proceeding to the courtroom where Peggy worked. In each instance the male kept his head down and we have no clear picture of his full face. The tapes did produce some partial profiles of his face and each day he wore the same clothing." Carr got photos made from the tape and they we're getting ready to interview all the courthouse personnel to see if this individual could be identified. Carr said, "The individual coming off the beach cannot be ruled out as being the same person videotaped in the court."

Carr relayed to Brogan, A detective with the University of Maryland campus police department talked with Peggy's boyfriend. In the campus detective's opinion, the boyfriend's reaction to the news was both genuine and triggered extreme grief. The boyfriend provided the names of seven students who could verify that he was attending a study hall during the hours in question. The detective continued to share that it was his intent for each student to be contacted for a face-to-face interview, and a full report covering all the interviews would be sent to your office as soon as possible. The detective believed the boyfriend was clueless as to anyone who would want to hurt Peggy and assured him that she had not mentioned a word to him about any fears coming from her employment. The boyfriend also denied that neither he nor she had any involvement with drugs or any other type of criminal activity and had no enemies that he was aware of.

Brogan's drive to Sandpiper on this sunny and crisp day would normally be a gentle ride through very flat, but beautiful farm country. The return trip over the Chesapeake Bay provides a breathtaking view. Traffic on Route 50 was light even as he passed through Easton and Cambridge and finally the outskirts of Salisbury. The rest of the drive was flat and straight to the Atlantic Ocean and Sandpiper.

Brogan was lost in dark thoughts as he drove mechanically, missing the scenery all around him. *Who is responsible for Peggy's death?* The evidence was already pointing towards the courthouse. A motive was not clear, because information gathered so far failed to find a reason, why someone would want to hurt Peggy. *Who is the person visiting Peggy's court room three days in a row?* The cases being heard during that time frame seemed to be insignificant minor offenses. No single defendant appeared in that particular courtroom on those three consecutive days. Brogan knew he was missing something. The thing that would tie the unknown suspect to the court and to Peggy. This was a mystery that needed to be solved before this criminal could strike again. Theories and possibilities tumbled through Brogan's mind. He needed a plan and brainstorming with his team. The clock was ticking, and Brogan felt in his gut time was not his friend. The assailant was out there making his own plans.

Lost in his thoughts, the first hour of his return trip passed before grabbing his cell phone and calling Carr again. Carr answered on the second ring. Brogan said, "I will be back in Sandpiper in about two hours. I'll meet you and Ryan at the courthouse. Bring the video and the photos so I can see them."

Brogan then called Chief Richards and briefed him, leaving out the detailed description of the knife and the potential of the surveillance tapes at the courthouse. What the chief didn't know he couldn't tell the mayor, who might tell anyone.

Brogan suspected it would take good old-fashioned gumshoeing to solve this mystery, but he was anxious to get to it. The killer was probably waiting for him somewhere in Sandpiper and Brogan was coming for him.

14

WEDNESDAY AT BECKY'S

As Brogan was driving back to Sandpiper, Lonnie was just waking up to start his Wednesday. Lonnie was at Becky's place and felt very safe and secure. Becky lay sleeping next to him. Her hair hid some of her face and shoulder. Her soft white skin was highlighted by the contrasting color of her hair. His loins began to stir at the sight of her. It would take a long time to make up for all his days behind bars. He was on the right track. He was invincible. He was a shadow moving through Sandpiper fulfilling his need for revenge. He was still on an adrenaline high. He felt good. He felt alive for the first time in years. Funny, how death of another person, made him feel alive.

Tuesday night had been a mixture of emotions for him. He was elated that he had been able to fulfill a longtime need to get even with those who had put him in a cage for ten years. Vengeance had been his at last. It was sweet. Vengeance was like a drug to Lonnie. He wanted to feel that rush again. The girl he left lying dead on the beach symbolized all those he held responsible, even if she personally had nothing to do with what had happened to him.

That fact she wasn't involved in his arrest and incarceration was eating at him. If her death brought him so much pleasure, he couldn't imagine the feeling he would have if he could strike at one or more of those who had actually played an active role in taking his freedom from him. It had been so easy. No one even knew he was lurking in the area planning to even a score that everyone else had long ago forgotten.

Lonnie had spent a great deal of time Tuesday night peeking out the condo window facing the beach. He had seen the police lights and activity, but it was too far away to actually see what they were doing. He resisted an overwhelming urge to walk down and pretend to be just an onlooker.

Hours passed before the lights were extinguished on the beach and things returned to normal. Lonnie noted the presence of headlights as they passed the condo he was able to identify a four-wheeled police vehicle now patrolling the beach. He laughed to himself, thinking that was like closing the barn door after the horse was long gone. Cops were so stupid and so predictable. Maybe he would find a way to taunt them and see how they liked being the ones under the gun and facing the ridicule of the public.

Sex with Becky on Tuesday had been less than spectacular and he debated with himself as to what he should do with her. She was definitely of no further value to him. He had her car and her cash and even her credit cards. She had filled a sexual need. Once he had set the rules she had complied with his every demand, which had been many. He would have to decide what to do with her. There was way too much stuff going on to make that kind of decision.

Around midnight Tuesday, there was loud and insistent knocking on the door. Becky was drugged and taped so she never moved, but he added tape to her mouth just in case. All the lights in the condo were off and Becky's car had been parked blocks away. Lonnie moved cautiously to a window facing the parking lot and peeped under a crack below the blinds. He observed what was obviously an unmarked police car idling in the alleyway behind the condominiums. The knocking stopped and he observed a white female dressed in slacks and a dark blazer move to the next condo door and begin knocking. Lonnie knew this had to be a police detective and was surprised that she was good looking and well-built for a cop. Her hair was up and he could see her face clearly when she stepped in front of her own patrol car headlights. She repeated the process at every condo door, but no one answered because no one was there except Lonnie and Becky.

Finding no one answering her knocks at any of these condos, the detective eventually returned to her vehicle and sat there for a few minutes writing something down. Lonnie knew enough about police work to know that they were conducting a door-to-door canvass looking for potential witnesses. Not getting an answer at the door did not mean they would not return. Lonnie would have to be extremely careful about lights in the condo and being seen coming or going from now on.

He did not recognize the female cop as someone he knew from ten years ago, but thought she would make another great target in his plan to get even. The fact that he could also have sex with her may have been driving his thinking about what made her a good target. Ten years without a woman was going to take a lot of making up. Becky had been a great start, but she was just the beginning. This was a reoccurring thought. It was driving his planning and actions. Was he obsessed with evil thoughts? No, he was seeking justice from those who had wronged him. This all made perfect sense to him.

Lonnie tried to recall the events at the time of his arrest and the face of a tall, dark-haired detective floated into view. This cop had been so smooth and friendly in his demeanor that Lonnie found himself confiding in him, and providing him with all the details of the attack on the beach. He told the detective he met this girl, named Gerri, and she had lured him into having a sex with her. She wanted rough sex, and he had tried to meet her needs. She had lied about her age, and never once said no or stop to what he was doing with her. He told the detective the knife had fallen from his pocket and she grabbed it. She tried to stab him and he ripped the knife from her grip and may have accidently cut her while trying to get away. He described Gerri as the aggressor who went crazy.

The cop had led him to believe that the girl had probably been responsible for what had happened to her, and if Lonnie just got it off his chest, things may go better for him when he eventually faced a judge. Yeah, he had been read his rights and knew what he said would be used against him, but being young and dumb, he talked without even being asked direct questions. The court had ruled his statements had been voluntary and unsolicited by the police. It all came up at his trial and Lonnie elected not to take the stand in his own defense. The little blonde bitch had sat up there with her scarred face and tears rolling down her cheeks telling lies about the attack. The jury went her way and he went to jail. That was the end of the story. Until now.

The tall dark-haired cop! *What was his name? Everyone who spoke to him during that period called him by a single name. Was it Brennen? Brenden? No, it was Brogan!* Brogan played a huge role in sending him to jail. Lonnie wondered if he was still around. A cop staying in a little burg like Sandpiper for ten years might be a stretch, but it was one thing that Lonnie had to find out.

Lonnie used Becky's cell phone and called 411 and asked for the general information number for Sandpiper PD. He then dialed the number and when a female voice announced he had reached Sandpiper PD, Lonnie asked for Detective Brogan. To his surprise the female said, "Let me check and see if he is in." Panicked by the chance that he may actually be talking to Brogan in the next second or two and that Brogan would recognize his voice, Lonnie terminated the call.

Lonnie realized that he had been stupid. Nobody is going to recognize a voice they haven't heard in ten years. But with Lonnie's luck, this fucking cop would, and Lonnie couldn't afford to make any mistakes when it came to Brogan. The risks versus rewards had just been escalated and Lonnie began to envision himself defeating this long-forgotten foe. Lonnie was older now, smarter now, and definitely a match for this aging cop. Revenge, sex, and murder were driving Lonnie and a confrontation with Brogan would be the ultimate rush. Lonnie thought to himself, *Brogan, you're out there looking for me, be careful what you wish for, because now I'm looking for you!*

15
BIG DECISION

Once a decision is made it's just a matter of execution. Lonnie took a long, hot shower. He washed his hair twice because it had become so oily with sweat and grime over the last few days. He shaved his face and brushed his teeth. He dressed in new jeans, shirt, socks, shoes, and underwear all purchased using one of Becky's credit cards. He would throw it away when he left Sandpiper so as not to allow law enforcement to follow him when he made his run to California's west coast.

Becky was awake and was asking to use the bathroom. Lonnie told her that she could use the bathroom and to take a shower and clean up because his work here was done. Soon she would be allowed to go home. He gave her no specific information about how this would happen, but she jumped on the idea and helped him remove all the duct tape from her wrists and ankles.

He allowed her to walk on her own to the bathroom and followed casually behind her. She entered the glass stall and turned the water on full force and at a temperature that started to steam up the bathroom. She did what he knew she would do. She tried to scrub him off every part of her. She cleaned herself inside and out, using both bar soap and body wash found in the bathroom. She let the water run over her in a constant flow that removed dirt, sweat, urine, syrup—and most importantly evidence. The cuts on her inner legs had already mostly healed; she had become so compliant with his demands that he had not cut her since Sunday morning. She spent a great deal of time cleaning her girl parts as if those being clean would remove the memories of what happened there.

When she was done, Lonnie moved quickly to the shower stall with a towel in his hand. She opened the shower door and was actually smiling for the first time in four days. Her eyes danced with the promise that her nightmare was coming to an end and she would soon begin the awesome task of forgetting this ever happened. She knew Lonnie would warn her not to say anything to anyone, but those words would be a waste of time. She had already made up her mind that she would never whisper a word of this to anyone. This horrible secret would go with her to the grave. She had been played for a fool and had paid a severe price. Reliving it with anyone would not change what had happened. She wanted to run home to her boyfriend and return to being the mouse she really was.

Before Lonnie handed her the towel he told her she had a lot of soap still on her back and she should probably rinse it off before drying herself. Becky reached up and reengaged the shower and the water poured out still warm.

She was about to turn her back to the shower when she felt her head snap back by the force of Lonnie grabbing a handful of hair and yanking it straight back and down. Becky saw

Lonnie's hand and arm move across her face and then retracted just as fast. Her eyes registered the bright red streak of water etching itself across the shower wall and glass. Water was pouring down her chest and for some reason she could not speak, scream, or even control her head. She raised her hands to her throat and her fingers seemed to slip inside a gaping hole. Now she was choking and coughing and felt like she was drowning in the shower water even though her mouth was clamped shut. Becky's senses dulled and her knees would no longer support her. She sank to the shower floor while her arms and hands tried to grip the shower walls to hold her up. Becky never comprehended that her throat had been cut and that she was bleeding out in the confined space of the shower.

Lonnie simply stepped back – amazed by the power of his knife. There had been no resistance and he had applied very little pressure. One cut and Becky was no more. No more witness. No more sex partner. No more problems.

He let the water in the shower continue to run. He reached in and removed the shower head on its flexible hose and washed down the arterial spray that marked the level of the initial cut. The bright red turned to pink and then to clear water. The bottom of the shower stall seemed to fill with blood, but it too would soon turn to pink and then clear water. Lonnie walked out of the bathroom leaving the water to run on Becky's body for the next hour. The rush had returned. Lonnie had killed two women and felt no remorse.

Disposing of the body presented both challenges and opportunities for Lonnie. He did not want to leave it in the condo because it creeped him out, but where would he put it?

The answer came to him with clarity and purpose. He would put Becky right where he had left Peggy. It would be dangerous for him, but if he could pull it off he would make the police look the fools he knew them to be. Maybe he could even flush out that tall detective who had done him wrong all those years ago.

B each patrols had continued since Peggy's death had been discovered, but like any other police activity, it was predictable. To the officer assigned, it was a boring waste of time. No killer is going to be walking up and down the beach where he had just committed murder. You just can't fix stupid and this patrol was stupid.

Lonnie timed the patrols and realized you could set your watch by them. The patrol vehicle was passing by the condo every sixty minutes. It was not exactly on the hour, but if it went by at 6:45 a.m. you could be sure it would return at 7:45 a.m.

An hour was all the time Lonnie would need to do what he planned. At 9:45 p.m. the patrol vehicle passed by the condo and then by the scene of Peggy's murder a minute later.

Lonnie was prepared. He had already moved Becky's car to within a hundred yards of the condo. When the patrol vehicle went by, he moved it to the condo, backing it right up to the door. He left the vehicle running and opened the trunk lid before entering the condo. He had already disabled the interior light in the car and removed the bulb from the light in the trunk. All the lights in the condo remained off and he moved quickly inside where he had staged Becky's body, wrapped in some extra bed sheets he found in the owner's closet. He lifted her easily to his shoulder and carried her out the door and dumped her into the trunk of the car and quietly closed the trunk lid. He closed the door to the condo and reentered the driver's seat of Becky's car. He drove the short distance to 18th Street, checked his surroundings, and backed the car close to the opening in the dunes. He sat for a few moments checking the area for potential witnesses. None were present, and in fact, the beach had not seen much action since Peggy's body had been found. The old man who used to fish every night had given up his nightly crusades and was now fishing only during the daylight hours.

When he felt confident he was alone, Lonnie quickly left the driver's seat after turning the vehicle off and putting the car keys in his front pocket. He went to the rear of the car and opened the trunk he had unlocked with the interior release. He knew exactly what he wanted to do and expertly reached in and rolled Becky out of the trunk and back onto his shoulder. Fear made Lonnie even stronger than usual and he easily carried the body through the opening in the dunes. It was extremely dark and he could see no one so he moved to the left and down to the area where he had killed Peggy. Without any formality or the least bit of caring, he dumped Becky's body onto the beach as close to the spot where he had left Peggy. He pulled the sheet away and left her nude body lying obscenely on the sand, facing the stars that dotted the seashore sky.

Lonnie rolled the sheet into a ball and carried it back to the car and threw it on the floorboards in the backseat area. He restarted the car and drove slowly away so as not to draw attention. He left the headlights off until he reached Ocean Highway, and drove the car approximately seven blocks to another apartment complex that contained quite a few cars for this time of the year. He put the rolled-up sheet in the trunk, locked the car, and walked back to the condo and awaited the excitement he knew would happen at 10:45 p.m. He had accomplished his mission in seventeen minutes from start to finish; he was beginning to think his commando-style behavior was going to change everything in his life and make those who opposed him mere bumps in the road.

When he returned to the condo, he again stroked the KA-BAR that had traces of the blood of two victims. Lonnie couldn't help himself as he felt a stirring. He was getting excited and liked the feeling. Killing was definitely addictive. The more you did it, the more you wanted to do it again. Wednesday night was still young and a drink would hit the spot. There were several bars within walking distance and if he came back later, he was sure the police carnival would be in full swing. He might even risk walking down to the beach to see the clowns up close. He couldn't help but snicker to himself.

16
FOLLOW THE LEADS

B rogan pushed the speed limits, ignored orange lights and every other traffic control device on his way back to Sandpiper. At 10:45 a.m. he was meeting with his detectives in a private conference room in the courthouse. Detective Carr had been able to clip and splice the relevant portions of the three days of surveillance tape into approximately twenty minutes of valuable tape. Brogan watched it three times before even commenting. Each time it showed a white male coming and going from the courthouse, but unlike others visitors to the court, this individual kept his face diverted from the ceiling-mounted surveillance cameras. Using the metal detector as a gauge, they were able to estimate his height at approximately 5'8" and judging by his build, he probably weighed between 170 and 190 pounds. His hair was brown, cut short in an almost military style, and his clothes consisted of a black hoodie-type sweatshirt, black pants, and black shoes. No logos could be seen on any article of clothing. Each time the subject proceeded directly to Peggy's courtroom without hesitation, as if he knew exactly where he wanted to go. The length of time the subject remained in the courtroom varied. The times never appeared long enough to have been a defendant or a witness testifying in any ongoing case. All the cases heard in that courtroom for those three days had been pulled and none of the defendants or witnesses called matched the subject's description or were unaccounted for. Video for the days preceding Friday had also been pulled and reviewed and the subject did not appear on any of them. If this was the suspect, then there was a good chance this thing may have started on Friday. The why was still a mystery. All the court personnel had been shown the photos taken from the surveillance footage and no one recognized him or could remember the subject, including the guys working security. Brogan noticed on all three days the subject moved swiftly through the metal detector. He seemed familiar with the fact that even the smallest metal item would set it off and cause him to be noticed or challenged by security. Most people don't get through the metal detector on their first trip into a courthouse without setting it off. This guy had been to court before! The surveillance video on the building near the dunes showed a similar looking male leaving the beach. Had he been stalking Peggy for three days? What was his motive?

It was now after 1:00 p.m. on Wednesday and Brogan needed to get on the street and shake up some of the local bad boys who may by now have information that would break this case. Somebody knew the guy from the courthouse video and Brogan was determined he would soon also know.

Detective Ryan's cell phone rang. A quick glance told her it was the PD so she took the call. The police communication's officer told Ryan they had a Pennsylvania State Police detective on another line saying he needed to speak with a detective as soon as possible. Brogan told Ryan to handle the

Pennsylvania situation while he and Carr would start beating the streets for information on Peggy's murder.

Ryan got the phone number of the Pennsylvania detective and called him while she was still at the courthouse. Detective Jason North said he needed help. He had been assigned to conduct a follow-up investigation on what he described as an "Endangered Missing Person."

A young Pennsylvania woman had been reported missing from her job site after failing to show up three days in a row. Apparently there had been domestic issues between the woman and her boyfriend and now she was gone and was not answering her cell phone. Her car was gone and her vehicle description had been broadcast locally with negative results. The police had entered the missing girl's apartment, but nothing was found indicating where she may have gone. Her purse was missing and there were no signs of foul play at the apartment. Her boyfriend had been interviewed and admitted they had a fight, but he claimed to have no idea of where she might be. His alibi for his whereabouts seemed to be holding up, but was still being checked out. A female co-worker had reported the disappearance. The missing woman has no family in Pennsylvania. The co-worker had told police the girl was distraught over her rocky relationship with her boyfriend. She had told the co-worker she needed time away from him so she could think and make up her mind what to do next.

The co-worker said that this conversation had occurred on Thursday and when the woman failed to show up for work on Friday she was not overly concerned and covered for her by saying she was ill. When the girl did not show up for work on Monday or Tuesday, the co-worker became frightened and concerned for the girl's well-being and called the police.

Extensive interviewing of the co-worker revealed that as part of their real estate business, they handled rental properties for a variety of clients. One such property is a seashore rental in Sandpiper, Maryland. The co-worker admitted that two consecutive winters she and the missing girl had borrowed the key and spent the weekend at the rental property without telling anyone. The women had agreed at the time that the condo was the perfect getaway spot because it was free and no one would know where they were. The co-worker had done a key inventory and found the key to the condo missing. The co-worker was fearful that what she had interpreted as stress might have been a deeper depression. She was afraid her friend may have done harm to herself or was in some other type of trouble at Sandpiper.

Detective North said the missing woman's name is Becky Marshall, age 23. North was asking Sandpiper PD to look for Becky Marshall.

Detective Ryan had been down this road many times. Women come to this beach resort, hook up with some other tourist or local, and spend the next week in bed. It usually ended when both sobered up and realized what they had was a case of "Lost in Lust." Consenting adults doing their thing. No harm, no foul.

Ryan told North that Sandpiper PD was handling the murder of a local girl and had limited resources, but she would look into it on Thursday, if North could send her a photo and full information on the missing girl's vehicle. North said he would package up a copy of everything he had and have it relayed to her. She would have it on her desk in the morning. North agreed that this was probably just some young girl enjoying her freedom and forgetting that others would be worried about her. North thanked Ryan for anything she could do and told her to call him regardless of the time should the girl be located.

17
BOYS IN BARS

It was time to get on the street and talk to the locals. Someone may be sitting out there with valuable information, but you need to be out there asking the right questions if you wanted them to come forward. In Sandpiper, the best place to find local information was in the local bars. Brogan told Carr they would have their work cut out for them.

Brogan suggested to Carr, we can cover more bars if we split up. They agreed that if anything looked promising they would hook up to pursue the lead together. There are lots of bars in this town and they decided they would work the ones closest to the beach first. Brogan took the bars on the even-numbered streets and Carr took the ones on the odd numbers. They would stop at 13th Street at the end of the boardwalk to review their findings before going further north. They each had a photograph of Peggy to show potential witnesses who may have seen her with someone.

One thing about bars in beach towns—they all have clientele year- round. Some regulars are ready when the doors open. The patrons vary from down-and-outs to retirees, locals, and tourists. The regulars may look like they're in their cups all the time, but they are observant and don't miss much when it comes to strangers or people who just don't act right. Getting these people to talk to the police is an art form that Brogan has developed over the years. Some local punks and thugs call these bars their home and protect their turf from any perceived threat. Most don't realize that Brogan has roamed the bars of Baltimore City where tough guys really are tough.

Brogan had visited two bars with nothing being learned and then he entered the Rusty Hook, a small dark, place with two pool tables and an old jukebox as its primary draw for customers.

The barmaid was a chunky blonde number with a friendly welcoming smile, but not a lot of brains working behind her bright, blue eyes. Brogan knew her and she knew Brogan so there was no dancing around; he got right to the point. There was a young local girl in the morgue and Brogan was looking for information. The barmaid said no one new had been in over the last week and the regulars were acting normally.

Three bar stools from where Brogan had perched to talk to the barmaid sat Tommy, an unemployed deck hand on local fishing boats. Tommy was already way too drunk to drive. Tommy was forty-three years old but looked older. He was wiry, inked, and bearing a few scars from previous bar fights. Tommy had probably seen the inside of more than one jail, but most likely only their drunk tank. Brogan's questioning of the barmaid had begun just as Tommy was finishing the bottle of beer in front of him. Tommy pushed the bottle to the rail, but the barmaid was now focused on Brogan and the bottle just sat there.

Tommy had no patience and tapped the bottle on the bar

a couple of times and glared at the barmaid who still paid him no attention. Brogan watched Tommy from the corner of his eye but stayed with his questions. Tommy stood up and closed the distance to where Brogan was sitting and said, "This is bullshit. I'm a fucking paying customer and because of you I can't get a fresh beer." Brogan remained seated, but turned to Tommy and said, "It might be a good idea for you to sit back down and the lady will get to you in just a minute." Tommy knew Brogan was a cop, but he felt being told to go sit down challenged his manhood. Tommy had checked his brains at the door and now balled his hands into fists and made a move to throw a sucker punch to the seated Brogan.

Brogan saw it coming and, with the speed that comes from years of practice, blocked the punch with his left forearm and delivered a game-stopping right hand to Tommy's gut. The wind left Tommy like a punctured balloon as he doubled over, retching up at least his last two beers. Brogan had anticipated that as well and moved his feet, allowing the expelled beer to splash harmlessly on the floor. Tommy seemed to be melting as he slowly crumpled to the floor, gasping for air.

Tommy has only one real friend in this world and that is Melvin who was playing pool when all this action took place. Melvin weighs in at about 230 and looks like a big old farm boy with arms and shoulders that would be the envy of any football player. Melvin didn't hear the conversation, but saw his good buddy Tommy going to the floor in obvious agony. Melvin moved from around the pool table with his stick held in both hands, drawing it back to create the perfect right handers baseball swing. Brogan had time to go for his gun, but it never occurred to him. He moved straight into Melvin vicious swing so that Melvin's arm was the only thing that would make contact Brogan's body. That never happened either as Brogan brought up both hands and blocked the huge arm and drove his right knee into Melvin's left thigh. Brogan then delivered an upper-cut punch to Melvin's solar plexus. The knee to the thigh had left Melvin's entire leg without feeling. Melvin couldn't support his own weight and fell to the floor near his friend. Both were gasping to breath. The fight was over.

Two down and none to go! If Tommy had any other friends in the bar, they ducked their face into their drinks and refused to make eye contact with Brogan. The entire incident had taken less than two minutes. Brogan told the barmaid to call for a uniformed officer and sat back on his stool to wait.

Both men would be taken to the station for assault on a police officer, but neither would be formally charged after signing affidavits that they had no interest in filing a complaint against Brogan or the department. Sober, neither man was a troublemaker, and they had already received their fair share of street justice.

The bar interviews continued, but no one had any information about Peggy's death and no suspects were developed. It was about 10:50 p.m. when Brogan and Carr got back together. They had barely reunited when their cell phones began to chirp at practically the same time.

The calls were coming from Sandpiper PD and the information was astounding even to Brogan. The beach patrol officer was reporting a body on the beach at the same location where Peggy's had been discovered just one day ago.

There had never been a serial killer in Sandpiper until now! What the fuck was going on?

18
CHAOS

The scene was chaotic when Brogan's car slid to a stop on the sandy street leading to the beach. Yellow police tape was hooked to the snow fencing lining the tops of the dunes. The fencing was there to secure the sand and the natural plant growth from the herds of tourists who would otherwise march right over it.

Powerful lights were pointed from the tops of the dunes toward the beach and ocean. Manning those lights and hand-held microphones were members of the local TV, radio, and print media. Unlike the first scene, this one was far from secret. Baltimore-based media would also be on its way to file reports on this developing story.

Brogan hadn't seen her yet, but he knew that Lynn Murphy would be among media. He knew he needed to keep fully focused on the victims and the murders, but his heart and loins were telling him that a clandestine rendezvous would soon be in the offing. He looked forward to it, but shook off the thought and ducked under the crime scene tape. He acknowledged the uniformed officer who was guarding the perimeter with clipboard in hand. He recorded the time and name of everyone who came into the crime scene.

Brogan worked his way across the soft sand to the more firmly packed sand near the water. Someone had erected a three-sided wall of protective, nontransparent tarp that was shielding the victim's body from the prying eyes lining the dunes. The beach had been closed to everyone north and south of the scene at a distance of one hundred yards or more.

Michelle Vickery, the local medical examiner, and crime scene technician, Sloane McCoy, were already working the scene. The body still lay nude on the beach. A folded sheet was on a nearby gurney that would eventually be used to wrap and then remove the body.

As Brogan approached, he noted that once again no usable footprints were near the body other than those being made by the crime scene personnel.

The victim stared unseeing into the starry night sky. Her head was tilted slightly back, revealing a gaping hole in her neck that was pretty certainly made when someone drew a knife across her throat. The body was extremely pale and did not appear to have any other major wounds. Brogan could see some slight scabbing at multiple points between the victim's legs. What caused those marks was unclear at this point.

Brogan's mind was churning as he evaluated what had occurred. No coincidence would have placed two murder victims in the same spot within days of each other. The killer was sending a message.

I'm still here.
I'm still hunting.
I'm smarter than you.

The killer was taunting the police and there was nothing to indicate this killing spree would end soon. Two young women were dead and, other than a possible sighting on some courthouse security video, there were no leads. Brogan was facing a real who-done-it and the reality of a serial killer. He was in deep shit and the pressure was building.

The throat-cutting was consistent with the "Big Knife" used on Peggy and other evidence already in play. Chaos and mayhem were loose in Sandpiper.

19
CROSSING THE LINE

On the dunes the crowd shifted from place to place, trying to gain an angle or a height where they could see the
body. Some of the first on the scene said it was a naked, white
girl. That incited additional interest from the males looking on.

Among those males was a guy with a Sandpiper Beach
baseball cap pulled low over his eyes. His hair was short and it
was difficult to assess the color due to the darkness behind the
bright media light. Lonnie did not press to see the naked girl.
He had seen her enough. He did watch with morbid interest
as the media talking heads interviewed other spectators and
solicited opinions about fear and what the police were going
to do to make Sandpiper's beach safe.

Lonnie made sure he stayed far enough back so that he
would not be drawn into an interview, but close enough to
know the crowd was growing more restless as curiosity was
quickly turning to fear. The fear was being fanned by the media.

Among the reporters Lonnie observed, one was particularly striking in appearance. She had a larger than average
crowd around her. She was a TV person and was apparently

broadcasting live from the beach. She spoke directly into the camera held by a male co-worker.

Lonnie edged closer and could hear her say, "My name is Lynn Murphy from Channel 7. Blah Blah Blah."

Lonnie knew this gorgeous creature was going to be talking about him and he wanted to hear every word, so he edged even closer. Lonnie didn't like what he heard. She used words like "brutal, sadistic killer with no conscience." She said she hoped the police would catch this person soon and put them in jail. She also said that dumping the body in the same spot was either an act of defiance or the work of someone with a very low IQ. She seemed to be intimating that the latter was most likely.

Lynn Murphy had just crossed the line and didn't even know it. She stood within feet of a killer who didn't like to be laughed at or thought of as stupid. She had moved herself instantly to the top of Lonnie's "I'm going to kill you" list.

Lonnie faded back into the crowd, but kept Murphy in his sights. His knife was tucked inside his pants and lay against his hip. His new long sleeve Grateful Dead T-shirt hid the handle of the knife. It seemed appropriate for the occasion.

If the opportunity presented itself, Lonnie would take her tonight. If not, he would conjure up a plan to take her somewhere else and then keep her for a while. He would show her the error of her ways and teach her how to talk about people – especially killers like him. All thoughts of leaving Sandpiper were gone. Game on!

Murphy and the other media types quickly lost interest when the body was removed from the beach. They began packing up their equipment. Police were fanning out looking for witnesses, but Lonnie stood even farther back. One young uniformed officer approached him, but before the officer could say anything, Lonnie said, "I just talked to one of your guys a minute ago." He pointed in the direction where other officers were conducting interviews. The young officer accepted this information at face value and moved on.

Lonnie watched Lynn Murphy help her cameraman place some items in the news van. Murphy walked away when the cameraman drove off. Apparently, they had come separately. The gods were smiling on Lonnie as he quietly shadowed his prey down an alleyway behind some condos. Her heels were clicking on the asphalt and her ass was twitching in perfect harmony. Lonnie began to close the distance.

Murphy appeared to be heading for a black Lexus that was parked near a dim street light. Lonnie saw a tall man standing near the rear of the car so he slipped into the shadows of a condo and watched.

Murphy walked straight to the man, glanced around and then kissed him full on the lips. He kissed her back, but it only lasted an instant before both stood back from each other. They gave the outward appearance of casual acquaintances. The conversation that ensued was too far away for Lonnie to hear.

His focused moved from Murphy to the man. Lonnie recognized him almost immediately. This guy is a cop. The same cop who had put Lonnie in jail—Brogan. What was a cop doing kissing a TV reporter? Lonnie surmised that Murphy was a shot of cock for the detective.

Lonnie's hatred for the cop raged to the surface and his hand moved to the concealed knife. He figured he could walk right up to them like he was lost or looking for information and then stick the son-of-a-bitch before he knew what was happening. Lonnie would then force the girl into the Lexus and take her with him to Becky's condo.

The cop reached to his belt and withdrew his cell phone and put it to his ear. At the same time, he lifted a single finger to Murphy, signaling her to wait one. The cop moved six or seven steps away while he talked. After several seconds he holstered his cell phone, said something to Murphy, and strode away like a man on a mission.

Lonnie relaxed a little and refocused on Murphy, who was now alone again. She was fishing in her purse for her keys as she moved towards the driver's door.

Fearing she would get away, he moved quickly and approached her from the rear as she was opening the driver's door. Without a word Lonnie drove Murphy's forehead into the doorframe with enough force to render her stunned; she began to lose her balance and footing.

He savagely pushed her over the center console and gear shift into the passenger seat and passenger well of the car. He scooped up her keys from where they had fallen and simultaneously pulled out his knife. Murphy's upper torso was in the passenger floor while her legs remained on the passenger seat.

Murphy began to stir and was immediately hit in the upper thigh by the man behind the steering wheel. He told her if she tried to sit up or screamed he would cut her bad. He brandished the largest knife she had ever seen for emphasis. Murphy remained down and quiet and thought about escape, but was wedged at such an awkward angle she couldn't even reach the door release. She prepared herself mentally to make a move when the car stopped somewhere. Her head throbbed with pain from the impact with the doorframe. She didn't think she was bleeding but feared what the large-bladed knife would do to her. The tires crunched along the side street where she had parked. She had gone from telling the story to becoming a part of the story. She was well aware of how it had already ended for two other women.

20
NOW YOU'RE THE STORY

It was approximately 12:50 a.m. when Lonnie pulled the Lexus right up to the door of Becky's condo, quickly assessing that no one was around. He reached across the seat and pulled Murphy from the passenger floor and back across the center console. She let out a little yelp as her hip and legs thumped against the gear shift lever. Lonnie used his strength to overcome the obstacle and slide her across the front seat and out of the car through the open driver's door. He brought her to a standing position next to him. She was wedged between Lonnie and the open door. She had a red welt across her forehead, her dress was torn, and one shoe was missing. Lonnie thought she still looked good.

He pressed the knife to her side so she could feel it. He strong-armed her to the condo door and again wedged her between him and the door while he fumbled for the key. The lock clicked and he pushed the door open with such force that they both fell forward into the living area.

Murphy had been in tight spots before. She had dealt with all kinds of out of control people while she was covering other crime stories and major events. She hoped her good looks and talent with words would give her the time and opportunity to get away. Her abductor was acting on pure adrenaline. She would need to calm him down.

Lonnie pushed Murphy through the living area and to the open kitchen where he forced her to sit on a kitchen chair. He continued to menace her with the knife only inches from her face.

Murphy appealed to him, "Please don't hurt me. You don't have to do this. I'm a reporter, and if you want I can tell your story, because I know you must have one. Just talk to me and help me understand why you're doing this. I won't try to run or scream. Let's just talk."

He didn't respond to her pleas. He reached to a nearby kitchen drawer and withdrew the roll of duct tape he had used on Becky. He used his teeth to unravel a long section of tape and then cut it with the knife. He quickly taped Murphy's arms to her sides by wrapping the tape around her midsection, arms, and the back of the chair.

Murphy cried, "I'll cooperate if you promise not to hurt me." He answered her by slapping a short piece of tape over her mouth and around her head. He then taped each ankle to the front legs of the chair and stepped back to admire his prize.

Lonnie could hardly contain himself as he circled the chair taking in his new play toy. This would be the best yet. He knew Brogan wouldn't mind sharing.

Lynn Murphy's bravery and thoughts of talking her way out of this were quickly diminishing, as she was now unable to move or talk. She forced herself to remain calm even as tears began to leak down her face.

Lonnie wiped away her tears with a dishcloth and told her it would be in her best interest not to resist anything he did. He reminded her that he had already killed twice, but lied and said the other girls died only because they tried to escape.

He told Murphy that she was the most beautiful girl he had seen in a long time and he would like to get to know her better. He clarified this statement by using the KA-BAR to cut open the front of her dress and separate the cups of her bra. He cut the dress off of both of her shoulders and soon she sat naked from the waist up. She was truly amazing to look at. Even taped, her long blonde hair shined with luster as it hung down past her shoulders. If this was a boob job, it was a good one because they didn't look like cereal bowls. The area surrounding her nipples was extremely dark and her nipples were totally erect. Her skin was flawless. She spent a lot of time at the beach during the summer months, because the outline of her two-piece bathing suit was still evident in the middle of December, making the vision even more exciting to Lonnie. He was too slow to think about a tanning booth that Murphy used frequently to keep her year-round tan.

He slowly cut away the bottom portion of her dress revealing her panty hose. They were transparent and Lonnie could see she wore no underwear. It took a little work, but soon they were gone too and she sat nude before him. There was cloth trapped under the tape around her wrist as well as some of her panty hose remained at the tape around her ankles. He decided it was better to leave it than to take the chance of having to re-tape her. The remaining tape and cloth was hiding nothing he cared about.

Lonnie continued to wipe away her tears and ignored the sobbing that was coming from under the tape covering her mouth. He had yet to touch her in a sexual way, but he was fully erect and ready.

Go slowly he told himself, it would be better. This was going to be so good! He would go put clean sheets on the bed and then take her where he could enjoy her. This would be her best news story. Too bad she would be the subject rather than the writer.

21

THE CHASE

B rogan thought they might have caught their first break in the case. The cell call had come from detective Ryan. She said she had stopped by the PD to pick up some extra witness interview forms when she saw the package from the Pennsylvania detective sitting on her desk.

Her curiosity drove her to open it immediately even though she knew it would be a back-burner item with all that was going on in Sandpiper right now.

The packet contained only five pieces of paper. There was the missing person report that was a two-page form. There was a separate handwritten interview of the co-worker. Another handwritten interview of the boyfriend, and a one-page summary of the missing girl's driving record and registration information. Clipped behind the reports was a 4x6 color photograph of the missing girl. Detective Ryan's mouth fell open. She couldn't believe her eyes. Ryan had just seen this girl lying dead with her throat cut on Sandpiper's beach. The file said the dead girl was Rebecca Marshall, known to her friends and family as Becky. Ryan grabbed the packet and headed for the door while punching in Brogan's cell phone number.

When Brogan answered she told him she had a positive identification on the new victim and filled him in on how she knew. Brogan told her to meet him at the scene so he could see the reports and the photograph. He would wait for her in his car.

Ryan pulled in next to Brogan's patrol car and rushed to his passenger door. When she got in she handed the packet to Brogan. She said she hadn't even had time to read the reports yet, but knew he would want to know what she had. Brogan glanced at the photo and verified she was the dead girl on the beach. He began scanning the report. He stopped at a portion of the report describing the location where the co-worker thought the missing girl might have gone. The address in Sandpiper was on the beach only two blocks from where they now sat.

Ryan was pinned to her seat when Brogan threw the car in gear and roared down the short street to Ocean Highway and made a right without stopping. Ryan looked at Brogan, but he was intent on his driving and made no comment about where they were going. Two blocks later he made another sharp right turn into 21st Street. Brogan told Ryan to call for back up. He spit out the address he had read from the report. Ryan knew the address, as she had just been there the day before conducting the canvass for witnesses to the first murder. No one had answered at any of those condos.

Brogan had never activated his siren during this short, but heart- stopping drive. He halted just short of turning into the line of condos. He saw one car parked directly in front of the address in question. How could it be? Lynn Murphy's car was parked in front of the suspected address.

Ryan became frightened as Brogan's face hardened, his eyes turning to flint and bored into the suspected address.

Brogan violently threw his door open and ordered Ryan to stay put and wait for back up.

Brogan moved like a cougar, completely focused on his prey, which in this case was the front door of the suspected condominium. Ryan was out of the car and moving behind Brogan even though she had been told to wait. Ryan knew something very bad was happening but lacked the information to know what.

Brogan knew about probable cause and about search warrants, but he also knew about exigent circumstances – and these were definitely exigent circumstances. Without breaking stride, he did a well-practiced front kick to the door near the knob. Beach condos were not meant to withstand frontal assaults and the door nearly disintegrated. His eyes took in the living and kitchen areas. His gun was now in his hand. Sitting naked and bound in a kitchen chair was Lynn Murphy. Her eyes were wide with fear and relief at the same time. He wanted to run to her, cover her, and work away her bindings, but he knew he had to clear the condo first.

He said to Murphy, "Is he still here?" and she looked like a bobble head indicating he was.

Glass broke somewhere in the condo and Brogan moved silently down a narrow hallway to several closed doors. He listened intently and heard noise coming from the room at the end of the hall. He kicked the door open with such force that it slammed against a wall and then flew closed again. In the brief moment that it was open he observed curtains flutter in the gaping hole that used to be a window. The suspect was in the wind. Brogan knew better than to stick his head out the window and retreated back to the kitchen area to help Lynn and seek reinforcements to bring this killer to ground.

Ryan was in the living room area with her gun in one hand and a portable radio in the other. Brogan could hear the sound of sirens growing louder by the second. He pulled off his jacket and wrapped it around Murphy and gingerly began removing the tape from her mouth and head. When she could speak, she couldn't. Her body racked with uncontrollable shaking and she sobbed deeply as Brogan wrapped his arms around her and tried to still her. Ryan looked on in amazement. She had never seen a police officer comfort a victim in this fashion, but it seemed to be working as Murphy quickly relaxed and quieted. Ryan knew who the victim was and grabbed her utility knife from her gun belt and handed it to Brogan so he could cut away the bindings from her arms and ankles.

"Did he hurt you?" Brogan asked Murphy. This is a routine coded question for "Did he rape you or sexually assault you?"

Murphy shook her head and then began shaking again.

Brogan again quieted her with his embrace and asked, "Lynn did you know him or can you describe him for me? We need your help right now so we can find him."

22
NOW THE HUNTED

S and and small shards of glass encased him, as he tried to
find his footing just below the bedroom window from
where he had jumped. The KA-BAR and canvas bag lay within reach as Lonnie struggled to his feet. The beach ran right
up against the condo building and being a first-floor unit had
given him a chance to escape. His heart pounded in his chest
and his eyes darted from place to place as his brain raced to
come up with an escape plan. He drew a blank and just began
plodding through the sand, trying to put distance between
him and capture.

In mere moments he had gone from raging passion and
lust to overwhelming fear. Lonnie checked himself over and
found no obvious injuries or bleeding wounds. He concluded
that only the purest of luck had afforded him the ability to
break out a window with the butt of the KA-BAR and literally fling himself through the jagged opening that once was a
window without doing serious bodily harm.

They would be coming for him now. They would put him
back in his cage and throw away the key. He had to run. He

had to get away or die in the effort. In that moment Lonnie made the decision that he would stop at nothing to remain free and if anyone got in his way they would pay the ultimate price. He had his knife and he had a small head start. Adrenaline surged back through his body, returning him to his Marine-Superman persona.

Lonnie hadn't actually seen him, but he knew it was Brogan who had fucked up everything. This guy was a worthy opponent who Lonnie would have to put down. Right now, the priority was just getting out of Sandpiper. He could lay low for a while and then return to finish his work of balancing the scales of justice back in his favor. In jail Lonnie had been a dead man walking with no direction or future. Now he was alive and emboldened. He was a force to be reckoned with, and soon everyone would know his story and fear his presence. He clutched his knife and bag and ran as fast as the sand would permit. Distant sirens were sending a message to his already frayed nerves to keep running.

23
SHUT THE ISLAND DOWN

Lynn Murphy was not your average victim. As an experienced reporter, she regained her composure far faster than most and was quickly giving Brogan a description of her attacker. Detective Ryan was writing notes, almost as fast as Murphy was talking, and then broadcasting the description to the onrushing police cars via the portable radio held in a death grip. Brogan turned from Murphy and told Ryan to close down the island.

Sandpiper is a very narrow strip of sand bordered on one side by the Atlantic Ocean, and on the other side by Assawoman Bay and the Saint Martin's River. The scenario of a felon on the loose in Sandpiper had been discussed and rehearsed in training sessions. Sandpiper was actually a peninsula with only three ways out. Two bridges in Maryland joined the mainland to the Sandpiper near its most southern point and again near the middle of the peninsula. A very narrow spit of land that bordered the State of Delaware lay at its most northern point. The most southern tip ended at the "Inlet" which was a stretch of water allowing boats to enter and exit the bay into the Atlantic Ocean. The Inlet has extremely swift and dangerous currents and would be nearly impossible to swim even in the summer. Winter passage would be a death wish. Two or three patrol cars at each bridge and the Delaware line could virtually shut down anyone trying to leave. Roadblocks could be established in a matter of minutes and then be reinforced to become fully manned checkpoints that no one could escape.

On the other-hand a water escape would present a multitude of problems for law enforcement. An equal amount of problems would exist for the fugitive if he did not know his way around waterborne vessels. Sandpiper PD had its own patrol boats. The Coast Guard, Maryland State Police, Sheriff's office and local fire departments also had watercraft that would be called in to create a picket line that would prove hard to pass through. This was December and it would be hard for Lonnie to find a boat in the water that was not a commercial charter or workboat. The smaller personal ski and fishing boats were populating the multiple storage yards in the area or up on their boat trailers awaiting the first warm breezes of spring, still months away. The winter had been mild and no ice had formed to provide escape by foot over the water.

Ryan called the PD via the radio and used a predesignated code word to alert the police communications personnel who in turn made the calls and notifications that would quickly isolate Sandpiper from the rest of the world. The net was closing on a killer.

Brogan knew his biggest problem was the thousands of apartments, condos, and motel rooms that were closed for the season but would offer refuge to a fugitive wishing to avoid apprehension. A manhunt unseen in this beach community was about to commence and there would be no retreat until the killer was in custody.

EMTs had arrived at the condo and were attending to Lynn Murphy who appeared no worse for wear and tear. A sketch artist was in route from Salisbury Police Department to help Murphy render a portrait of the man who would be the target of this manhunt. Crime scene technicians were also arriving to conduct an examination of the condo that was now suspected to be the killing ground used by the suspect to kill Becky Marshall.

Phones of law enforcement personnel from all over the Eastern Shore of Maryland and southern Delaware were ringing cops and support personnel out of bed and onto the streets to confront a growing crisis of fear gripping an area that beforehand was known to be a place where you went to relax and have fun.

24

HIDEY HOLE

Lonnie knew he had only minutes to get off the beach and the streets before the dragnet would close over him. He left the beach cutting between some darkened condo buildings and made his way to Ocean Highway. Flashing red and blue lights could be seen coming north towards him, but so distant that he knew he could cross without being seen. He pulled himself together long enough to make his crossing a casual stroll so as to not draw the attention of anyone else who may look his way. On the other side of the highway he quickly moved to the darkened areas of other condos and apartment buildings. Most building were currently shut down for the winter but a few were occupied. He considered breaking into a car and seeking refuge in a backseat, but he knew that would offer very little long-term security. He began scanning the vast number of darkened windows trying to calculate the chances of breaking into one of the vacant buildings and then hold up until the heat died down.

Lonnie moved two or three blocks closer to the bay and away from Ocean Highway until he came to a large complex of wooden condo buildings. This place gave the overall appearance of needing repair, painting, and cosmetic upgrades. There were no elevators, but dozens of staircases going in all directions. The buildings were three stories tall with units facing the streets, the parking lots, and small manmade parks with slides and monkey bars for children. The playground equipment was also old and in need of paint. Weeds grew up between cracks in the chipped painted concrete around the playground area. Lonnie assumed the disrepair would extend to the security aspects of living in such a place. Surveillance cameras were doubtful. Door and windows locks would also be old and lacking. Within seconds he had made his way to the third floor of a building facing a parking lot. He knocked on the door to Unit 314, but no one answered and no lights came on. He forced the door lock using his K-BAR and entered a dark and rundown condo. He stood perfectly still listening for sounds of life and found none. He moved to a large window facing the parking lot and opened the blinds just enough to allow nearby streetlights to illuminate the room in a dull yellow light. Threadbare rugs and furniture from the 80s decorated the room. The kitchen appliances were stuff you'd see on Antique Road Shows, and the stale musty smell of disuse permeated Lonnie's nose.

There were good and bad in his surroundings. The good was that it appeared no one had been here in quite a while and it was just as likely that no one would be coming. The bad were that he could find no food in the ancient refrigerator that was as warm as it was empty and no food supplies in any of the cabinets or closets. The power was turned off at some location Lonnie couldn't find. It was cold and damp in his new hidey-hole and survival here would not be easy. Moving around outside while a massive manhunt was underway was not an option. Lonnie found lots of blankets and pillows so he gathered them together in the living room area and placed them close enough to the window that he had a little bit of light and the ability to watch any activity around his building. It would be daylight soon and he would have to stay put until darkness returned. Just the thought made Lonnie's stomach turn with hunger and his tongue thicken from lack of water. Even tough guys in jail got their three squares a day. Badass with a big knife didn't carry much weight against hunger and thirst. Lonnie curled up in his nest of blankets and fell asleep. Later today he would make a new plan that would allow him to drink once more from the sweet cup of vengeance and then he would put this one-horse town in his rearview mirror forever. Lonnie slept like a baby with his knife still loosely clenched in his fist.

25

I KNOW THE KILLER

As the sun peaked over the fog of a December ocean, the word was out that a killer was loose in Sandpiper. The local radio and television stations were hammering away with tidbits of information both real and rumored that were making the unknown suspect seem more than human. He had disappeared without a trace from the hundreds of police officers who still combed the streets hoping to get a sighting or a break.

The sketch artist had rendered a picture of what most people were describing as a clean-cut looking white guy with a short military-style haircut and no visible scars or tattoos to aid in his identification. The sketch was being shown almost constantly on both local and Baltimore area news channels, hoping someone would come forward and say "I know that guy." What no one knew was the sketch didn't really look like Lonnie. Lynn Murphy's strategy to stay alive had included not making direct eye contact with her tormentor. She felt that he might consider it a challenge to his manhood.

Murphy had made a concentrated effort to keep her eyes

diverted and assume a position of submission in hopes of gaining his sympathy and avoid his wrath. The strategy was never fully tested, but it did make her observations far from accurate. She settled on a likeness that was too vague for a true identification and would probably lead to multiple mis-identifications.

No one is more interested in crime than criminals. The jail does not serve to keep the inmates uninformed, but rather crime is their lifeblood and they love to hear someone is out there making the Pigs look bad. Two homicides and a possible serial killer with a large knife was the only topic this morning in the Maryland penitentiary.

Except for one cell where Billy Ray Snelling sat in deep thought. He was thinking about his old cellmate, Lonnie Harris, who had said he had unfinished work to do in Sandpiper. Lonnie Harris – who had visited his mother on the day he got out of jail. Lonnie Harris who, if you used a little imagination, could be the guy in the sketch being shown over and over again on the dayroom television. Lonnie Harris who had absorbed every word and technique Billy Ray had shown him about using a very large knife. Lonnie Harris who was the only guy who knew about Billy Ray's stash.

Billy Ray sprung from his rack and exited through his open cell door and went down the short corridor to the dayroom where other inmates gathered to watch TV and play board games and cards. Billy Ray went to one of the correctional officers who he respected for his treatment of inmates. He asked him if he could make a phone call to his mother. Phone calls are normally allowed only in the evenings and only one a week unless there was a documented emergency. Billy Ray told the officer that he had forgotten today was his mother's birthday and she would be leaving for work soon and he would not be able to reach her if he did not call her now.

The officer had no way of checking at this hour of the morning to confirm the truth of Billy Ray's story, but Snelling seemed so upset he had forgotten, the officer felt sorry for him. He took Billy Ray down the hall and un-locked a door to a small room that housed telephones that inmates were allowed to use. Letting an inmate make a phone call was not a violation of any jail protocol and was often used as a way of gaining jailhouse information from a grateful inmate. The officer said the only condition under which he would allow the call was to let him dial the phone to verify Snelling was calling his mother. Snelling agreed and held his breath as his home phone number was dialed. The officer identified himself and asked if he was speaking with Mrs. Snelling. Billy Ray could not hear the response, but the officer said, "Your son wants to speak with you." Billy Ray was handed the phone and the officer stepped from the room while lifting two fingers to indicate two minutes only. The officer positioned himself near the window in the door to keep Billy Ray under observation. With the door closed he could not hear what was being said.

Billy Ray said, "Mom, please don't ask questions. Just run up to my room, move the foot of my bed to the left, and lift the short piece of floorboard with the little knot hole and tell me what you find." Billy Ray heard the phone being placed on the table and then nothing. About one minute passed and Billy Ray carried on a conversation with himself saying he was sorry he had forgotten her birthday and that he loved and missed her. Billy Ray stopped talking when he heard the phone being lifted from the table. "Billy Ray," his Mom said,

"There's just an empty hole. There's nothing in it." She continued to talk, but Billy Ray had already hung up the phone. That motherfucking Lonnie Harris had ripped him off.

It took only a moment for Billy Ray to see his get out of jail free card. He immediately started beating on the door and announced the second it was open, "I know who the killer is!"

26
COULD THE ID BE THAT EASY?

Brogan had finally gone home to catch a few minutes of shut-eye around 3:00 in the morning. What the hell was that buzzing? Brogan opened one eye and watched his cell phone dance across his nightstand. Memory cells started clicking and he remembered setting his phone on vibrate. From sound asleep to wide-awake took only a moment and the phone was pressed to his ear. "Brogan," he mumbled.

The police communications officer told Brogan he had the Maryland penitentiary on the phone and an assistant warden was reporting he might have the name of the killer being sought in Sandpiper. Brogan asked to be patched through and after a few clicks the connection was made.

The assistant warden said his name was Jeffrey Clawyer. He told Brogan an inmate was reporting he knew who was doing the killings in Sandpiper and for favorable consideration of an early release he would give it up. Brogan asked Clawyer to isolate the inmate and said he would find a state's attorney and be in route to the prison. Clawyer agreed to that arrangement and put the inmate in isolation. The time was 7:00 a.m.

Brogan knew that many cases were turned on information provided by inmates and arrestees who took knowledge and turned it into favorable leverage to benefit them. Brogan also knew that no deal could be made without the state's attorney's office being involved.

Worcester County, Maryland, is not a hotbed of crime and therefore the state's attorney's office is small. Three full-time attorneys and two part-timers handle all the cases coming to the office from the multiple police and enforcement agencies working within the county. Brogan knew them all and had them all on speed dial. He picked Maria Christian. She was full-time, young, aggressive, and would do the right thing to help catch this killer. She also lived close to Brogan and he could swing by and pick her up on the way to the prison.

Christian picked up on the second ring and was quickly briefed in on the situation. Christian told Brogan she had several violation of probation hearings scheduled for the afternoon, but she was clear for the morning. She said she would be ready to go in about fifteen minutes as she was already preparing to leave for work. She told Brogan she would call Rudy Carol, the state's attorney, and inform him what she was doing just to cover both their asses. Brogan was fine with that, but made sure Christian knew he had no time to waste. He would be in front of her place in exactly fifteen minutes.

Brogan pulled to the curb in front of Christian's residence in twelve minutes. His eyes were bloodshot and his face unshaven. His clothes were fresh, but there was no tie or attention to detail. Both were Brogan trademarks. Christian didn't disappoint as she literally flew down her front steps before Brogan could put his car in park.

No words were exchanged as Brogan pulled quickly from

the curb and raced towards Route 50, the main road to the Bay Bridge and prison that lay beyond. This would normally be an approximately three-hour drive. The trip was completed in two hours and forty minutes. On the way, Christian told Brogan that she had spoken with State's Attorney Carol and had been told she could use her own discretion on making any deal that would result in identifying the killer.

B rogan and Christian had been here frequently and knew the routine of getting inside the prison. Both were known to all but the newest of correctional officers. This combination reduced the entry time down to minutes and soon they stood in the office of Assistant Warden Clawyer.

Clawyer said a correctional supervisor reporting a strange series of events had called him. First an inmate had approached a correctional officer begging to call the inmate's mother because it was her birthday and an early morning call was his only chance to reach her. The correctional officer had relented to the request and allowed the phone call to be made, but verified the call was being placed to the inmate's mother. After a brief conversation with his mother the inmate had begun banging on the door demanding to speak with the warden. The inmate insisted he knew who was doing the killings in Sandpiper and would reveal the name if a deal could be made to allow him an early release.

Clawyer said the inmate was Billy Ray Snelling who was serving time for several armed robberies in the Salisbury area. Clawyer reported that he had taken the liberty of pulling all of Snelling's files and reviewed them, pointing to a stack of documents on his desk. Clawyer said today is not the birthday of the inmate's mother, according to the records. Visitor logs revealed only monthly visits by Snelling's mother. There was a father's name and an older sister listed as potential visitors, but neither had ever visited the inmate.

Clawyer handed Brogan a report summarizing the crimes committed by the inmate. No one had ever been hurt during the commission of the robberies, but all had been threatened by the brandishing of a very large knife. Never a believer of coincidence, Brogan knew he was looking at the thread that would tie all these odd facts and circumstances together. Brogan shared the report with Christian and she immediately grasped the importance of this information.

Two dead, Murphy kidnapped and assaulted, the entire Eastern Shore in an undeclared state of lockdown. Would it be this easy? Was someone just going to tell Brogan the name of the person so many people were searching for? Brogan held his optimism in check. Too many things were hinging on an interview with an already convicted asshole.

27

CAN MOM HANDLE JAIL?

B rogan asked Clawyer to arrange for a room where he and Christian could interview Snelling in privacy.

While this was being done Brogan used the warden's phone to call Salisbury PD. He spoke to Detective Beverly Walker. Brogan told her things were breaking on the murders in Sandpiper and he needed her help. Brogan asked Walker to go to Snelling's mother's home in Salisbury and find out what had been discussed during the call her son placed to her earlier this morning. Anticipating a protective mother, Brogan asked Walker to push her hard if necessary and make it clear that she may be involving both herself and her son in an obstruction of justice in a least two homicides if she withheld information. Walker assured Brogan she would get the information and call him as soon as she knew what was discussed. Brogan's cell phone was currently stored with his weapon and car keys at the prison's entry point, so he gave her Clawyer's office number and alerted him to the importance of any call from Walker.

Christian called her office and asked State's Attorney Carol to pull all the prosecution files on Billy Ray Snelling. Christian asked him to check in particular the status of the knife used during the commission of his robberies. Christian told him they were about to interview Snelling and she would call Carol as soon as it was concluded.

It took about ten minutes to move Snelling from his confinement location to a suitable interview room. An inmate talking to cops and state's attorneys was not seen in a favorable light by other inmates who see such activity as a betrayal. Those same inmates would do the same exact thing given the chance. The hypocrisy of this kind of thinking was completely missed by these predators.

Brogan and Christian were guided down a multitude of narrow hallways to arrive at a solid steel door with a small window in it. These hallways had kept them from the eyes of the general population who would be hooting and hollering if they had seen these two intruders from the free world. Brogan glanced in and saw a metal table bolted to the floor. Two bolted chairs faced a single bolted chair on the other side. A large steel ring was mounted on the table directly in front of the single chair. Brogan knew this ring would allow a short chain connected to handcuffs to pass thought it. The inmate would be unable to move his hands more than a few inches and would be kept in a seated position. Behind the single chair was another solid steel door. This would be where the inmate would enter the room, closely guarded by at least two correctional officers.

This was clearly a room used solely for law enforcement and prison officials to conduct interviews. Normal visiting areas kept inmates and visitors separated by thick bulletproof glass, and talking was done through telephone handsets hung on the wall on each side of the glass. Those visiting areas provided no opportunity for physical contact.

The door on the other side of the room opened and an inmate was ushered into the room flanked by two huge men wearing correctional uniforms. These stern and muscled guardians of the internal peace of the prison dwarfed the inmate. The inmate was placed in the chair where handcuffs on a short chain were threaded through the steel ring fixing him in place. The man now seated and shackled in the room was well-nourished, medium length brown hair. He had dark brown eyes that were already darting around the room in expectation. He was inmate-pale from being incarcerated for a long time and he currently had no facial hair or other identifying features. He leaned forward in his chair and appeared anxious to begin this meeting.

While Brogan's face filled the small window, it was clear the inmate was unable to see him. Obviously, this window was made of one-way glass permitting a view in, but not out. Brogan studied the inmate closely. Snelling's eyes continued to shift from side to side, always returning to the door where Brogan stood, anticipating it to open. Snelling was on the small side and it was clear that he would be too small to commit a strong-armed robbery. The use of a weapon to threaten would be necessary. How could this little shit know what was happening in Sandpiper unless his mother knew something and had shared it with him. Didn't make sense, but nothing else was making sense either. Brogan moved away from the window and allowed Christian to have a look. Christian looked briefly and turned to Brogan and said, "What do you think? What's our plan?"

"He called us," Brogan replied. "Let's see what he has to

say. No deals until he tells us something we can check out. He needs to know if he tells us a single lie, there is no deal."

Christian and Brogan agreed they would step out of the room and discuss any deal before agreeing to anything. Time was wasting and a killer was out there, still killing. "Let's do this," Brogan said as he turned the door handle and entered the small interview room, closely followed by Christian.

Snelling sat straighter in his seat, hoping an erect posture would help sell his importance. It was all he could do while cuffed and seated. Brogan and Christian took their seats. Brogan introduced Christian as an assistant state's attorney and himself as lead investigator in the Sandpiper murders.

Snelling said he had the name of the killer and he wanted to be released from jail if he gave up the name. He said he only had two years left on his sentence. He wanted the deal in writing before he said another word.

Brogan's steely blue eyes burned holes in Snelling. Brogan made it very clear that there would be no deal unless Snelling told them something that made this meeting even worthwhile. Brogan reminded Snelling that he had called for them and they could just stand up and walk out and leave him rotting for another two years.

Brogan played a card he wasn't sure would work, but it also might be the thing to move this negotiation quickly forward. Brogan asked Snelling, "Has your mother ever been in jail?"

Clearly confused, Snelling violently shook his head in the negative because words would not come. Brogan continued, "This morning you brought your mother into this and if she lies to protect you we will lock her up for obstruction of justice in two ongoing homicide investigations. Is your Mom strong enough to endure time in jail while we sort this out?"

Snelling's ticket to freedom had been turned into a possible incarceration of the one person who had always stood by him. "Okay, okay," Snelling whined. "I'll tell you what I know if you leave my mother out of this and maybe help me a little with getting out of here sooner."

Christian spoke up and said, "Tell us what you know and I promise if it's good I'll go to bat for you. If it results in the arrest of the right guy I'll work to get you out of here. One lie to us and you've got nothing and you can get on your mother's visiting list while she's serving time."

Shaken to the core, Snelling was about to start babbling when a sharp knock came at the door at Brogan's back. Brogan knew this would be important. He held up his hand to Snelling and told him to think about what Christian had told him, especially the part about lying. Brogan rose from his chair and exited the room, but not before directing Snelling to remain silent until he returned.

Clawyer stood in the narrow hallway. He told Brogan he had a message from Detective Walker. Walker says that Snelling's mother told her that a deputy called her this morning and then put her son on the phone. Her son had told her to go to his bedroom, move his bed and pull up a floorboard and tell him what she found. Mrs. Snelling told Walker she had never known about this hiding place, but when she lifted the board, the space was empty. As soon as she got back on the phone and told her son she had found nothing under the floorboard he hung up on her. Mrs. Snelling swears she has no idea what is going on.

28

CONFESSION IS GOOD FOR THE SOUL

Snelling was told to slow down more than once as he gushed out his story of his cellmate betraying him. Billy Ray told Brogan and Christian that he had been housed with a guy named Lonnie Harris. Snelling said they had become friends, leaving out the part about being sexual partners. Billy Ray said Lonnie was crazy and obsessed about being wronged by the cops, court, and women in general. He said Lonnie frequently talked about getting even, but was never specific in what he meant. He often spoke of getting even or taking revenge or seeking vengeance against those he perceived had done him wrong. Harris had even talked about being wronged by his mother as a child and then even more so by her dying and not being there when he needed her to get him out of jail. Billy Ray summed it up by saying there were times when Harris was just a scary dude to be around.

Over time Billy Ray said he revealed a lot about himself to Harris. This included his arrest for robbery and his eventual incarceration. During those discussions it came out that Billy Ray had a stash of unrecovered loot hidden in his mother's house, under a floorboard in his bedroom. Lonnie also learned that the robberies were enabled by the use of a large knife and that knife was also hidden with the loot.

Snelling said the knife and the power it had given him to overcome all resistance merely by being displayed intrigued Harris, who had told Billy Ray the only reason he was in jail is because he had used a small knife. It had failed to do the job and allowed a living witness to manipulate a jury into thinking he was a bad person.

Lonnie Harris asked probing questions about the knife and where Snelling had gotten it. Snelling said he may have bragged a little bit about being in the Marine Corps and being issued a KA-BAR and taught how to use it in combat situations.

Snelling explained that days in jail were long and boring and Harris urged Billy Ray to tell him about his Marine Corps training, and especially about the use of the knife. Snelling said it all seemed so innocent at the time and it helped fill the long hours of confinement. He described the use of the toilet paper roll as a make-believe knife and the repeated drills on using it to Brogan and Christian. Snelling said the use of camouflage and concealment were also hugely interesting to Harris.

As Billy Ray told his story, Brogan could see the direct correlation between this story and the crimes that had been committed. The use of the KA-BAR and the stalking for the purpose of revenge for perceived wrongs all made sense. If Lonnie Harris had not been a disturbed personality when he entered jail he certainly was now. Brogan was sure the video of the male in the courthouse was that of Lonnie Harris as he sought his target. Why Peggy was selected was an unanswered question as she would have been only a child when

Harris went to jail. Brogan suspected it had more to do with her position in the court and more particularly that specific courtroom, as it was the only one visited by the suspect.

Brogan theorized the other victim had been one of opportunity or just being in the wrong place at the wrong time. The condo on the beach placed Harris where he needed to be to formulate his attack on Peggy. Becky Marshall was just a tool Harris used and then threw away when no longer needed. Lonnie's attack on Lynn Murphy was not as easy to understand, but Brogan's gut told him it was personal and was directed against him as much as Murphy.

The moment Brogan had heard the name Lonnie Harris it set off distant memories of a case he had been involved in many years ago in Sandpiper. Snelling's description of why Harris was incarcerated brought it all rushing back: the young stabbing victim found on the beach and her tale of horror at the hands of an equally young sexual offender who did not hesitate to use lethal force to terminate his victim rather than face apprehension.

Brogan recalled the interview room at the police department and the young offender telling how the victim had brought the violence upon herself. He said she had enticed him to have sex with her, lied about her age, and then pulled back and laughed at him. In his mind, she had gotten just what she deserved and asked for. Brogan had feigned understanding and sympathy. He made extensive notes he would later use in testimony to put this demented and unremorseful offender away before he could hurt anyone else. The rest of the details of the case remained in a gray area of Brogan's mind. The old case file would be the source to bring it all back into focus.

Brogan's aversion to coincidence also told him his meeting with Murphy at the crime scene just moments before her kidnapping was why his gut was telling him this was personal.

Snelling concluded his story by telling Brogan and Christian that Harris had begged for his help when it came time for a possible early release on parole. Billy Ray said he had been duped into talking his mother and his uncle into providing Harris with the needed address and employment opportunity necessary for release. Before walking out of jail Harris told Snelling he had a few things he wanted to do in Sandpiper before he took off to the West Coast. Snelling said there was never any intention on the part of Harris to adhere to his conditions of release, but he had never told Snelling he was going to hurt anyone. Snelling said his mother had told him that Harris had stopped by the house to thank her for allowing him to use her address and had remained for only a few minutes. At the time Billy Ray admitted he thought that was a nice gesture, but now realized it was just a ruse to get into the house and gain access to the stash.

The crimes in Sandpiper involving a court employee, the use of a knife in the killings, and the vague resemblance to Harris in the sketch being shown on television caused Billy Ray to make up a story to talk to his mother and confirm his fears that he had been ripped off.

It was clear to Brogan that Billy Ray Snelling could care less about these victims or what Harris was doing in Sandpiper. Billy Ray was motivated only by the fact that Harris had taken his loot, his knife, and made Snelling look the fool he was.

Brogan had heard enough and knew he had to get back on the street to lead the search. He told Christian he wanted to take a short break and they went into the hallway. Brogan said he believed everything they were being told about Lonnie Harris and briefly recalled to her the investigation roughly ten years ago. Christian had not been a states' attorney at that time and had never heard of the case.

Brogan said he had to get back to Sandpiper to pull all this together and asked Christian is she could stay and take Snelling through the story one more time, seeking any additional details that might lead to where Harris may be hiding or people he may contact in Sandpiper who would assist him avoid apprehension. She agreed and said she would make her own arrangements to get back to Sandpiper. She said that States Attorney Rudy Carol had already told her not to worry about her afternoon court appearance, as that would be reassigned.

Brogan left her and went back to Clawyer's office to bring him up to date before leaving. Clawyer said he understood and told Brogan that Rudy Carol had called for Christian and left a message that he had pulled the Snelling prosecution files and learned that the weapon used during the commission of those crimes had never been recovered. Brogan knew who had the knife, but not where it was. He could only hope that the knife would not be used again to end another life before Harris could be found and taken down. Before leaving the prison, Brogan obtained the photograph taken of Lonnie Harris at the time of his release. One look told Brogan this was the guy and it was his responsibility to end this reign of terror.

Brogan had seen many cases turn in an instant and that is what had just happened. An unidentified killer now had a name, a photo, and a motive – however distorted it might be. It still did not answer Brogan's main question: where was

Lonnie Harris and where he would strike next? Sandpiper had been shut down so quickly Brogan believed he was still in town and that he presented a clear and present danger to everyone else he may encounter. Brogan felt a mix of helplessness and frustration, but he also felt a growing determination that time was running out for Harris. Brogan set a new personal best for the time it took him to get back to Sandpiper.

29

OPPORTUNITY AND OPTIONS

The music was soft and soothing to his cramped and chilly body. It was a great dream and he tried to stay asleep so it wouldn't stop. Lonnie came to full consciousness slowly, but the music didn't stop. He was still cramped and chilly, but the soothing music continued to flow. His head was resting against a wall. Blankets and towels encased his body, providing some respite from the penetrating cold.

The music wasn't part of a dream, but rather coming from the wall where his head rested at an uncomfortable angle. He straightened and pressed his ear to the wall. No doubt about it. Music was coming from the other side. It was probably loud music being muted by the thickness of the wall. A newer condo would have had sufficient fireproofing and insulation to make this impossible.

Someone was next door and that meant food, drink, and possibly car keys and other resources Lonnie would need to make his escape. Opportunity was knocking, and he had two options. Capitalize on the opportunity or stay hunkered down and avoid possible confrontation. Lonnie had his knife, but he knew he could encounter multiple male residents or even someone better armed.

Hunger and thirst won out and Lonnie unwrapped himself from his nest. He stretched to get his blood flowing. He needed a shave and he needed a shower, but far more important was his need for food and drink. He went into the bathroom to relieve himself and then studied himself in the mirror. He finger combed his hair into place and straightened his wrinkled clothing as best he could.

His plan was simple. He would hide the knife under his shirt, go next door, and see who answered the door. If the opportunity was there he would overpower the person or, if need be, kill them outright. If there were too many of them or the person seemed capable of defending themselves, Lonnie would opt to ask some mundane question and then retreat to his condo to reconsider his options and make a better plan.

Lonnie placed the knife inside his pants on his right side with the scabbard unhooked so he could easily draw out the knife. He let his shirt drop over the handle and examined himself in the mirror. If you weren't looking for it, the handle of the knife would go unnoticed. Lonnie stepped from the condo onto the open decking that served as the hallway in front of each of the condos on this floor. He checked the parking lot area and saw no one walking around so he moved to the condo marked 312. He pressed his ear to the door and could hear the music better. He tapped lightly on the door, intending the sound to be transmitted only to the occupant of 312. Nothing happened. Lonnie now knocked louder and waited. The music decreased in volume and the doorknob began to turn. Lonnie's hand instinctively went to his right side as if he was a cowboy getting ready to draw his gun. Realizing his mistake, he let his hand drop farther down on his thigh and tried to assume a nonthreatening posture.

The door began to swing inward and jerked to a stop as an interior chain held it from fully opening. Brown eyes and very dark hair surrounded an angelic face full of curiosity filled the narrow opening. She was short and Lonnie could see over her head, but the two-inch gap allowed very little view of the interior of the condo. Lonnie was drawn back to the face when she said, "Yes?" The yes had ended with a question mark leaving Lonnie scrambling for something to say.

"Hi," I'm your neighbor and I don't have any power. Do you have power?" It was a dumb question with the music still playing in the background, but all he could come up with at the moment. Poor planning, Lonnie thought to himself.

The angel on the other side of the door didn't seem to notice and answered, "Yes, we've got power."

Lonnie hung on the word "we" and backed away from his instinct to just shoulder his way into the condo by breaking the cheap chain that was keeping him on the wrong side of the door. "Maybe it's a breaker," the angel suggested, her eyelashes partially shrouding her coffee, brown eyes.

"I just got here and I don't know where the breakers are," Lonnie said, hoping to be invited in to be shown the location of the breaker box.

Angel eyes turned her head slightly, raised her voice and said, "Sara, where are the breaker boxes in these condos?" Lonnie tensed at hearing there were two girls and was again considering his options. Lonnie heard a voice, but not the words. "Check in the last cabinet over the stove," said the face at the door. "Okay," Lonnie said. "I owe you one."

"No problem," she said pushing the door closed. He heard the lock engage.

Lonnie quickly retreated to his condo to lick his wounds at having been out maneuvered by a dark-haired angel who remained just out of his grasp. He wondered what Sara looked like. Probably ugly; good-looking girls always traveled with a cockblocker. It didn't matter as the girl at the door would be well worth Lonnie's attention, and if Sara was a loser, she could be dealt with or used as leverage to get what Lonnie wanted.

He was still hungry and thirsty, but found the breaker box where Sara had said it would be. The main breaker was in the off position. Turned on, Lonnie would at least be warm while he schemed and fantasized about his next sexual encounter. The spigots also produced water now, but it was running rusty brown and smelled far too foul to drink.

Every time Lonnie felt his time in Sandpiper was running down he found a reason to ignore the dangers of staying. He could work this out. He just knew he would prevail. He needed to keep planning his next moves carefully and his stay here would become legendary. From seemingly nothing he had grown into this larger than life villain that was capturing media attention while striking fear in the hearts of many. This town was just full of opportunities and options.

30

THE GIRLS NEXT DOOR

Sara was dripping water as she walked from the bathroom towards the front of the condo. She wore a towel wrapped around her wet hair and nothing else. Unabashed by her own nudity, she saw Tanya standing with her back pressed against the door of the condo.

"Who was that?" Sara asked. "Don't know. Guy next door," Tanya responded, absently. "Said he didn't have any power in his condo."

"Was he cute?" Sara inquired mischievously.

Sara and Tanya were definitely Yin and Yang. One was light and one was dark. Both were drop-dead gorgeous and knew it via any mirror they passed or any guy they met. Sara was as aggressive as Tanya was reserved. Under the towel Sara's hair was long and blonde. Her eyes were so bright, a shade of blue most thought they were contacts, but they were not. Sara was a natural blonde, which was clearly evident in her current state.

Tanya's dark hair and eyes perfectly contrasted that of her best friend. Apart they were strikingly beautiful. Together they were Fantasy Island in high heels. Neither could remember the last time they had purchased a drink or paid to get in a club. They were both Juniors and were preparing to go into their senior year at the University of Maryland. For as long as they could remember, Tanya's grandfather had given them the keys to his condo in Sandpiper. It was sort of old and the building was a little rundown, but the free accommodations couldn't be beat, and once they drove off the parking lot in Sara's Corvette, they owned this beach town.

Seeing Sara naked no longer had a shock factor for Tanya as they had seen each other naked since they were young girls sleeping over at each other's houses. Tanya had tried to turn the tables on Sara by walking around naked, but Sara was so liberated she didn't even notice.

Sara was a party girl who had slept with half dozen or more guys already, but Tanya had had only two lovers, and she had been in love with both when it happened. Currently, both girls were unattached and liking it that way.

They had one steadfast rule that had kept them out of trouble throughout their teenage years and early adulthood. If they went out together they would come home together no matter what. If they met someone they liked while out at night they would never leave with that guy. If he was for real he could show up the next day in broad daylight where both girls would further vet him. Both had pledged to remain single until Mr. Right came along. Mr. Right would be good looking, never married, have no children, and be employed with a future. He also would have to come from a family that was stable and rich. Rich had just recently been added to their wish list as they saw some of their girlfriends struggling to make ends meet because they married some guy who came from nothing and was going nowhere fast—or at least not fast enough for Sara and Tanya.

"Tell me about our neighbor." Sara pushed for more information. Tanya said, "He was just a guy. Brown hair cut short like a soldier or a jock. Kind of rumpled looking like he didn't own an iron. Think he was hoping to get invited in, but that wasn't going to happen."

"Rich people can be frumpy dressed you know," teased Sara. "But being frumpy and staying in these condos is two strikes against him. Could you tell if he had a big package?"

Tanya's face turned a little pink as it always did when Sara asked her sexually oriented questions or accused her of being a cocktease. "Didn't look," Tanya retorted and went to the couch to resume her reading and listening to one of the music stations on the television. "Where do you want to go tonight, Sara?"

"How about a pub crawl?" Sara suggested. "We can go up to the Delaware line and work our way south until we get back here. There are a lot of spots we can go. If we hit and run we can get free drinks and not get cornered by any guys just looking to get laid. After one drink we'll tell them we have to meet our boyfriends who are taking our kids to the amusement arcades. Once we say we have kids and boyfriends they're usually glad to see us go."

"I hate lying to guys, but you're right about them backing off at the mention of kids." Tanya giggled and said, "I'm in!" Tired of listening to music, Tanya switched to a local station. She threw the remote on a nearby chair and watched some home improvement show coming to an end. Before the station went to commercial there was a teaser saying there was breaking news on a serial rapist and killer being sought by local authorities.

Nothing takes the fun out of being at the beach more than crime reports of rape and murder. Tanya reached for the remote and turned off the TV.

31

I'M WAITING FOR YOU

The sound of laughter leaked into the darkened condo. Lonnie became alert and moved close to the front window to get a peek. The laughter was pure and generated by female voices. The exact words or cause for laughter was lost, but the spirit of friendship and good times was clear, even to a cynic like Lonnie.

From the sliver of window Lonnie allowed to be his view of the outer world, he saw double gorgeous. One blonde, one dark, and both dressed to the nines and sporting bodies to die for. The dark-haired girl was the one who had answered the door for him, and the blonde must be the girl she had spoken to while Lonnie remained locked outside. Lonnie wanted both of them without hesitation and his mind began to churn with desire.

He could hear their heels as they clattered down the wooden stairs. The laughter continued as they reached the parking lot. Lonnie took a chance and opened the condo door and moved toward the railing to see where the women were going. They walked toward a forest-green Corvette with a tan convertible top. The blonde moved to the driver's side and the brunette approached the passenger door. In a split second they were both inside and a second later the engine engaged and the car left the parking lot with the chirp of the rear tires as the driver applied power and popped the clutch. The vehicle turned toward Ocean Highway and was gone.

Lonnie began to think about how he would add these two women to his list of conquests. Not the smartest guy in the world, he still possessed the natural evil to contrive a means to achieve his personal goals.

Knowing the girl's condo would have a similar lock on the front door as to the condo he currently occupied, Lonnie decided he needed to get inside while they were gone. Perhaps he could set a trap. It was already growing dark outside so he would use the cover of darkness to his advantage.

Lonnie left the cover of his condo and with knife in hand moved the short distance to the next condo. Just in case there were still other occupants he knocked gently on the door; there was no response and no sounds coming from inside. He made quick work of the lock and was inside within seconds. Before closing the door, he examined it and saw only a few small scratches left by his knife. He felt sure they would go unnoticed when the girls returned home. He closed the door and stood perfectly still for a few minutes, letting his eyes adjust to the darkness. In his jailhouse training he had been told about night vision and how you could see much more than you thought if you just let your eyes adjust. Small nightlights shone from rooms down the hall and partially illuminated the hallway.

The condo was a mirror image to his condo. Lonnie had no problem maneuvering the space. He raided the refrigerator that was fairly well-stocked. He made sure he took only small portions of everything so it wouldn't be noticed. There were twelve bottles of beer in the refrigerator so he drank two of them, refilled them with water and rotated them to the back of the refrigerator with the caps placed snuggly back on top.

When he had diminished his hunger, he began exploring the rest of the condominium. There were two bedrooms. Both smelled of the women who occupied them. He rummaged carefully through their clothing and placed various articles to his nose so he could enjoy the very essence of their being. The bras and thongs were of special interest to him and his demented fantasies. He searched for money and credit cards but found none. The jewelry appeared to be costume and of no value. The bathroom was loaded with shampoos, soaps, perfumes, and girly stuff he didn't even recognize. He did find compacts containing pills that he assumed were birth control. In both rooms he found small vibrators, both pink and both fully charged. Must have been a two for one sale for party girls?

He checked the closets and areas where he might conceal himself and wait for the girls to come home. The closets were tiny and would offer no concealment if the doors were opened. No place to hide and no way to escape. What if the girls brought home some guys they met? Could be trouble for him if he had to deal with four people at once, especially if the guys they picked up were jocks who could handle themselves despite his knife.

An alternative plan formed in Lonnie's mind. The back bedroom was the largest and had a sliding door that opened onto a small wooden deck large enough to hold a small table and maybe two chairs. Currently it was empty. He slowly opened the slider after unlocking it and peered out. He saw a similar deck that came off the back of his condo. It would be easy to move from one deck to the other. There was a single light fixture on each deck and neither was lighted. Lonnie reached up into the globe of the light on the girl's deck and loosened the bulb a couple of turns and then hit the switch on the wall and nothing happened. He then drew back into the condo and closed the slider, leaving it unlocked. He figured when the girls got home they would lock the front door and throw the deadbolt and chain lock, but would they check the rear slider they already knew was locked? He doubted it. His plan would depend on this oversight.

Lonnie then adjusted the blinds hanging over the sliding door so that they were cracked open just enough so he would be able to see into the bedroom from the deck. He took a chance and went out on their deck and made sure he would be able to see in and opened the slider paying special attention to noise. It was an old condo but a very quiet slider. Good news for him. He moved to the bed and looked at the blinds trying to see out onto the deck. In the darkness he couldn't even make out the railing around the deck. Any additional light in this room would just make it more difficult to see out.

The trap was set. He would return to his condo and wait for the girls to come home. Once he was sure they were locked down and alone he would move from his deck to their deck. He would wait until the girl in the back bedroom was asleep and then he would make his move. He was confident he could surprise and overcome the first girl without even alerting the other girl that there was a problem. Once the first girl was bound and gagged he would move to the second bedroom and repeat the process. Once both women were incapacitated, he would spend the next few days enjoying the fruits of his labor. He could not repress a low chuckle at how clever he was and how he continued to be several steps ahead of all those who sought to bring him down.

He would leave no witnesses, only a town with a lot of dead women and a cop who couldn't find his ass in a closet. Lonnie wished he had been able to complete his adventure with the cop's girlfriend, but as his jailhouse training had taught him, you must remain flexible and improvise. His loins began to throb with anticipation.

Lonnie's entire plan depended on him being patient. Not easy for a guy who had already spent ten years waiting to show everyone who was in control? The minutes turned to hours and the night passed slowly for Lonnie who was coiled like a spring waiting to be released. Around 1:15 a.m. he heard tires crunch on the loose gravel at the entrance to the parking lot. Lonnie had cracked his window just enough to permit the night sounds in. The sounds had warned him of the many police cars patrolling the area, undoubtedly looking for him.

This time the sounds came from the tires of the dark Corvette. It parked in almost the exact same spot and the doors swung open and the girls reappeared. Still looking good and still laughing. The laughter was now hushed and personal, like they were sharing a private joke they didn't want Lonnie to hear. No hulking men emerged from the Corvette and no additional vehicles joined theirs in the parking lot. They moved towards the steps and soon the heels again clacked their way toward him. Lonnie thought for a moment he should abandon his plan, leap out and drag them both into his condo as they passed his door. No, no. There would be screaming, scratching, kicking, and a chance one or both would break away and bring the wrath of hell down on him. Cops were everywhere and they were just waiting for him to fuck up. No, his plan was solid—just be patient.

The girls passed and Lonnie heard the lock click next door and the door open and close. It was so quiet he could even hear the deadbolt engage and the slight rattle of the chain lock being placed in position.

At 2:00 a.m. the soft sound of music playing next door told Lonnie the girls were probably in for the night. Now it was just a matter of time and he was primed and above all patient! Well, not too patient. Fifteen minutes passed and Lonnie had already let himself out onto his own deck with his Marine bag full of goodies to make the girls cooperate. Lonnie could see there was now some light coming from the back bedroom. He moved to the railing to make his crossing. He thought to himself, *hey girls, where have you been? I've been waiting for you.*

32

LOVE MAKING DONE RIGHT

L onnie landed like a panther on the adjoining deck, crouched and remained perfectly still, listening to see if his arrival had been detected. Nothing happened. No one screamed. No one ran to the slider and looked out to see what was going on. Slowly Lonnie began to uncoil and move to t he small portion of wall next to the sliding door. His dark clothing would serve him well while he waited for his moment to strike.

Very slowly Lonnie moved just his head toward the slider to peer into the bedroom. At first, he was unsure of what he was seeing. A small light was lit on a nightstand next to the bed. It was so dim it was almost like candle light, but it didn't flicker. His eyes adjusted and he was able to make out a figure in the bed. Covered with a sheet, but not still. Now, moving slowly, but in such a fashion she appeared to be slithering or dancing to an unheard melody. He caught a glimpse of dark hair splayed across the pillow near the headboard. What the hell was she doing?

The more he watched the more confused he became. Her

shape was almost grotesque and disjointed and then the sheet slipped away to reveal it was not the dark-haired girl and it wasn't the blonde-haired girl. It was both of them in bed together, both of them nude and wrapped into each other in an embrace that spoke of deep passion and surrender. The blonde was kissing the breasts and belly of the dark-haired girl whose head was thrown back and her mouth slightly opened emitting a low, but guttural moan of immense pleasure. The blonde moved down between the legs of the dark-haired girl.

Holy shit. Lonnie had never seen anything like this, at least not in person. He had seen a couple of lesbo porn tapes before going to jail, but they had been very vulgar and aggressive. This was totally different and it turned him on more than anything ever had. He had witnessed guy-on-guy sex more than he wanted to admit and had been on both the giving and receiving end, always violent, rushed, and unfulfilling. This was different.

This was a slow grinding sex that looked as if both were trying to outdo each other in giving the other pleasure. There was no rushing, no pounding, no demands or reluctance. Lonnie was witnessing sex that really was lovemaking, and in his opinion, it was being done right. The rapture seen on the faces of the two girls supported his belief.

Lonnie did not know he was witnessing a secret that Sara and Tanya had shared since they were teenagers. It started as experimentation and had grown into a deeply committed relationship allowing both women to have loving relationships with men, but also allotted them the sheer pleasure of best friends sharing their most intimate secrets.

Being bisexual had permitted both girls their sexual awakenings in varied circumstances. This was one of the reasons neither was allowed to bring a guy home during a first meeting. No matter how turned on they became while being hit on and courted by men they met in their travels, they always found a far fuller release of sexual pleasure in each other's arms. No wham bam thank you ma'am for these ladies. They never woke up the next morning with that coyote-ugly situation, regretting an alcohol-fueled bad decision.

Lonnie was ready to rip the door off its track, charge into the room and throw himself on both women, thinking they would love to have a hard cock to share. He quickly reconsidered and realized he would enjoy watching and then enact his plan and become an active participant in an all-night fuck fest. To enter now would still result in screaming and unnecessary violence. These girls were beautiful and he would hate to have to cut them up just to gain control. *Patience will win the day. Just be patient, Lonnie!*

The women continued their lovemaking for what seemed like an eternity. They were giving Lonnie a firsthand lesson in how to please a woman. Eventually, both seemed sated and curled into each other. Soon they would be asleep and Lonnie would be on them.

The dark-haired girl stirred and disengaged from the blonde. She was getting out of the bed. Probably going to hit the head or smoke a cigarette before calling it a night. She would have to pass within inches of the slider on her way to the bathroom, so Lonnie pulled back a couple of inches just to be safe.

Suddenly the blinds came fully open and a naked girl stood for a moment looking out at the empty deck. Her hand moved to the lock and Lonnie heard the lock engage and his plan crash to a stop with that same sound. So, astounded by what had just happened, Lonnie moved from his hiding place and came face-to-face with the nude woman. Her eyes widened as if she couldn't believe what she was seeing, but clear recognition registered in the next moment as her eyes traveled from his face to his hands. In one hand he held the KA-BAR. It was a fearsome sight straight from a slasher movie. The blood-curdling scream that came next made the hair on Lonnie's neck stand straight up and his heart stand still. His free hand grabbed the handle of the slider and he pulled, but it didn't move. The blonde had now joined in the screaming and it was still reaching a crescendo when Lonnie launched himself off the deck and back onto his own.

Lonnie ran straight through his condo and out the front door and down the steps to the parking lot. He had the canvas Marine bag clenched at his side as he ran for his life.

33
SURVIVAL

Lonnie had barely cleared the parking lot when he heard sirens that seemed to be coming from all directions. He tried to stay in the darkened areas as he moved south towards downtown. Even though it was about 2:30 a.m. he was sure he would find enough activity downtown to blend in during closing time at all the local bars, restaurants, and pubs. Flashing red and blue lights converged on the neighborhood; if even one person spotted him and put out the word, he was done.

The first patrol car arrived at the scene in less than three minutes of the call coming from two very panic-stricken women. Brogan arrived on the scene in seven minutes and immediately took control. He quickly learned what happened and had officers check the next condo. The slider and front door were both standing open and marks on the front door suggested a break-in. Headquarters had already identified the owner. On the phone from his home in Newark, he told them there should be no one staying in his condominium. The owner lived in Delaware, but was in route to file a report with the police and determine if things had been taken. He assured the police there were no weapons in the condo and very little of value that may have been taken. Police gave the owner a description of the suspect and threw the name Lonnie Harris at him. The owner denied knowing Lonnie or ever hearing that name before.

Brogan ordered the saturation of patrol for a ten-block area surrounding the scene. He also called for a bloodhound to be summoned to the scene to begin a track. Detectives Patty Ryan and Bob Carr were on the scene with a map to set up permanent posts in addition to the roving patrols. Brogan would not let this guy get out of this dragnet. It would end tonight and it would probably end violently, as Harris showed no signs of letting up or getting out of town. Brogan warned all the officers via the radio to consider this guy armed and extremely dangerous. No one was to take any chances, and any sightings were to require immediate and overwhelming back-up. Tonight, people needed to use every bit of the training they had ever received to be safe and go home to their families.

Eight blocks away, Officer First Class Mary Jo Caudill, a seven-year veteran of the force, was assigned to a fixed post. With her was Officer Terri Johns with only six months on the job. The first five months had been in the police academy. Caudill was responsible for mandated field-training of Johns and so far, it had gone well. Johns followed orders and responded well to directions and constructive criticism. Now for the first time, Johns was given the responsibility of driving the patrol car and was doing a good job. Caudill decided that she would leave Johns behind the wheel. If anything were to happened while they were in this fixed post, it would allow Caudill the ability to move more freely. Johns had never been exposed to anything like this and was showing signs of nervousness as the two officers watched for any movement in the areas close to where they were parked. They were located between the scene and downtown, trying to prevent the suspect from going any further south. They were parked on the bay side of Ocean Highway and tucked between a building and a dumpster so the roller they were driving wouldn't be too conspicuous. They had already discussed how they would respond to any encounter with a suspect. Error on the side of caution, guns out and up, commands crisp and clear so there could be no mistake as to who was in charge and what needed to be done. Above all other things, stay in sight of one another no matter what.

Lonnie had made his plan too. No going back to jail. Kill or be killed without reluctance. No surrender. No negotiation. Lonnie only hoped that Brogan would get close enough to feel his blade. The net had tightened quickly and he was afraid to go any further. Four blocks from the condo and hunkered down in a crawl space under a house that was very old and unoccupied. The police were relentless with their roving patrols and spotlights illuminating the darkest of places. Lonnie had been lucky so far, but he knew it wouldn't last. He had to move. Keep going south – it was his only chance. He was now leapfrogging from spot to spot as soon as a patrol car would pass. It was slow going.

Brogan went over the story with the girls a few times and each time he felt they were leaving something out or holding something back. Why was Tanya in Sara's room? Tanya said Sara liked to wake up to the natural light of the sun coming up so they always opened the blinds before going to sleep. Tanya had admitted she was naked when she opened the blinds and flicked the lock. Again, that didn't make sense. Brogan could see that Sara was the more aggressive of the two girls. Sara was wearing a man's tee shirt with obviously nothing under it. On the other-hand Tanya was wearing a flannel gown pulled tight to her neck.

Brogan thought there might have been other witnesses who had fled the scene before the arrival of the police. He didn't have time to fuck around with these college girls. He singled Sara out and ordered her into the second bedroom. Because of the way she was dressed he had a female officer come into the room and stand inside the door. Brogan made it clear to Sara that even the smallest lie or withholding of evidence or information would lead to life-changing consequences for her and her friend. Brogan said, "You are holding something back. Tell the truth now or you're both going to the station." Sara thought for a moment and looked Brogan square in the eye and said, "Me and Tanya were going down on each other in the back bedroom and that asshole was probably watching us the whole time. It's not like we're gay. We just swing both ways. We do guys too and we just like to mix it up from time to time." It made sense now and Brogan didn't much care if they were having girl-on-girl sex. If Sara had been trying to shock Brogan with her crude description she had failed. Anything goes at the beach! Brogan had seen it all before.

He left the room and glared at Tanya who was now curled up in a ball, knowing full well Sara had given up their secret and probably relished the idea of doing it. What the fuck? They were still alive and the danger was such a rush she knew Sara would want her again tonight and she would welcome a second go-around, with the doors locked and the blinds completely closed. Might be the reason why none of their boy-girl relationships ever lasted.

Brogan could hear the baying of the hound. The dog handler was a county deputy, but there was a written and signed agreement allowing sheriff's personnel and the Maryland State Police to function within the city limits when invited in by the town in pursuit of a felon or in the case of a declared emergency. Seemed like all three situations were occurring tonight.

A new-looking baseball cap had been found on the floor in the adjoining condo and there was every reason to believe it belonged to Lonnie Harris. Brogan ordered the deputy to put the dog on the scent.

The dog was presented with the hat to sniff and then the dog went crazy. Pulling at his leash with his nose sweeping the ground in front of him. The dog pulled his handler across the parking lot. The direction was south and Brogan and two other uniform deputies were right behind the dog handler. Brogan notified all units that they were on the suspect's trail and he had initially gone south. Detective Carr radioed all units to hold their positions and monitor the chase. Radio silence was ordered so that no radio traffic would cover Brogan's messages.

Officer Caudill tensed and told Johns to stay focused. Their car was facing north so there was every possibility the suspect may come directly at them. Caudill said she would keep her eyes on the immediate front and right and Johns should stay focused on the area to the front and left.

Lonnie was six blocks south of the condo when he heard the baying of the bloodhound. No dark place would save him now. To survive he would have to take the initiative and be aggressive. He broke cover and darted south towards his destiny.

34

CONFRONTING THE POLICE

Officer Johns' eyes were aching from the concentration. She had already been shocked when a red fox had trotted across the street in front of them only twenty-five yards away. Red foxes were common in Sandpiper and were helpful in holding down the feral cat and rodent population that once threatened portions of the city. The fox population was not intimidated by the tourists, but remained hidden during the daylight hours. Foxes ventured onto the beaches in the evenings and had been reported sitting near the tennis courts watching early morning play as if it were someone's pet dog waiting to be taken home. Animal control officers frequently trap them and remove them from the city and release them in more rural settings to maintain a manageable population.

Officer Caudill told Johns to stay calm and just stay focused. Caudill had been on similar stakeouts many, many times and not once had she been in the right spot at the right time. The thing that made this different was that the suspect had already proven his pension for murder. A confrontation with him could go very badly if he obtained even the slightest advantage. Seatbelts were undone and both officers sat with their gun hands resting on their weapons.

Brogan and his team of hunters followed closely behind the bloodhound which seemed to be on a very strong track. Several German shepherds had been brought into town but were being held in reserve in case a more aggressive search was required. The shepherds would be used for building searches or, if the suspect was cornered, they could be sent in to dislodge him with minimum risk to human personnel.

The bloodhound had stopped several times at locations that were probably used by Harris as resting points or hiding places before continuing south. The pace was steady, but far from a run. Brogan scanned the buildings, trees, and other potential hiding places just ahead of the dog, looking for traps or ambush potential. Brogan worried for the officers south of his position. These officers were good people with all the training required to do the job, but none had confronted this type of danger before. Normal police calls for them were do-mestics, drunks, disturbing the peace, drug overdoses, and in-toxication. Assaults involving police normally entailed people similar to the ones Brogan had put down earlier in the Rusty Hook.

Brogan's past experience as a Baltimore City detective and his martial arts training prepared him well for just this type of situation. He just needed to run this bastard to ground and put an end to this small city horror story.

Another fox caught Johns' eye near a wooden garbage corral located approximately thirty yards away and to their left. Or was it a fox? There had definitely been movement – or had there been? Johns' eyes were almost popping out of her head and she stared at the spot where she thought she had seen movement. Without turning her head, she told Caudill she thought she saw something near the garbage corral to her left. Caudill shifted her attention to the area in question, but saw nothing. Both officers were now getting just a little jumpy and anxious as they continued to monitor the chase moving in their direction.

The old condominium complex where Lonnie had hidden had been turned into a command post and Ryan and Carr were coordinating the movement of vehicles and personnel. As the chase moved south, they had directed the more-northern stakeout units to collapse and move slowly south, tightening the net behind the suspect should he try and backtrack to the north. One block at a time, the units were forming a wall of blue firepower. All were anxious to get in on the fight. Everyone's adrenaline was surging and they had to call on their discipline and training to control their actions and maintain their positions as directed.

Chief Richards had been notified of the manhunt and had driven to the command post to lend his support to the efforts of his officers, and to be the eyes and ears of the mayor who had also been notified of the intense activity occurring in his city. Political fortunes are sometimes made or lost during these types of events, even though the mayor had virtually no control over what was happening on the street.

The mayor and Chief Richards had long ago reached an agreement that what worked best was to leave Brogan alone and not question his decisions or actions. He had never failed them before and both men trusted that Brogan was the man for this job. Chief Richards stood quietly off to the side as Brogan's detectives moved the troops around and Brogan took the point position in the chase.

There it was again. Not so much a movement as a change in the shadows inside the garbage corral. Johns told Caudill there was something in that garbage corral and she was going to check it out. Caudill said, "No you're not. Not alone. We do things together and our orders were to have backup. We will check it out and have each other's back while we do it." Not wanting to abandon the parking place that hid their car or illuminate their headlights that would also give away their position, they were left with using their flashlights that were in reality five-cell steel clubs that emitted light.

Caudill studied the garbage corral that was approximately sixty feet away and saw nothing. The corral doors stood partially open and large rubber garbage cans could be seen inside. The fence was approximately six feet high. It seemed impossible that anyone would have been able to enter the corral without being seen. A fox on the other hand could easily leap to the top of the corral in the back and then drop inside to search for food. Neither officer knew of the abandoned vehicle parked next to the backside of the corral.

"Okay, we go now, but we do it safe," Caudill ordered. Both officers exited the police car and moved cautiously toward the garbage corral. Caudill thought they should call this in and wait for additional backup, but it was probably nothing anyway and bringing in a bunch of trigger-happy police to look at a fox would be humiliating for years to come. Women in a police role are always trying to prove themselves in a male- dominated career. Trying to gain acceptance. What would my male counterpart do? Radio silence had also been ordered and was considered a priority. Caudill rationalized her decision was reasonable under the circumstances.

Lonnie had moved slow and cautious, staying as low to

the ground as he could while still moving south, taking short breaks to catch his wind. He had approached the back of a fenced-in area and saw a car backed right against the fence. The car had flat tires and bore the dirt of abandonment. Lonnie stepped on the trunk and peered over the fence. It was a garbage corral and large rubber garbage cans stood inside. A couple had their lids up and the smell was rank. Perhaps that's what Lonnie needed. Maybe if his scent were mixed with that of rotting garbage the dog would become confused or lose interest. It was worth a try, so Lonnie rolled over the top of the fence and dropped silently into a rear corner of the corral.

Before messing with the garbage, Lonnie peeked out the front of the corral through the partially opened doors. Sixty feet away sat a darkened police car, wedged between a building and a large metal dumpster. Shit. He was trapped. Scaling back over the six-foot fence was close to impossible and doing it without making a lot of noise or without being seen impossible. Lonnie pulled the KA-BAR from his bag and held it in his hand and did the only thing he could think of. Wait. Maybe the cops would move on. Lonnie shifted from foot to foot trying to think. The sounds of the dog approaching were just starting to reach his location.

Other sounds caught his attention. Car doors opening. The cops were getting out of their car. A quick peek near the hinge of the door told him it was two lady cops and they were moving toward him. He tensed and waited. The sound of footsteps grew louder as they drew nearer. This was it. Do or die.

Both Caudill and Johns had trained in clearing rooms, so they approached the corral as if it was a room in a house. Caudill was on the right and Johns on the left. Neither of them fronting the door until both stood with their backs against the fence. Both had their guns pointed up at face level and would extend them straight out in front of them as they breached the opening to the corral. Caudill would go in first and she would go in low, covering the left side of the corral for potential danger. Johns would go in a split second later and she would go in high, covering the right side of the corral for potential dangers. Caudill nodded her head and both officers executed their moves.

Lonnie stood with his shoulder against the inside wall of the corral next to the door opening. He held the KA-BAR in both hands above his head. His plan was simple – strike.

Caudill scanned her area of responsibility and saw nothing. Johns came face-to-face with Lonnie. Rather than shoot she made the rookie mistake seen so often in television shows and in movies. The word "Freeze" got only half way out before Lonnie drove the point of the KA-BAR between her ballistic vest and her neck. The blade completely severed the carotid artery. Lonnie did not have to pull the knife out as Johns' weight pulled her to the ground and removed the knife from her own body. Her gun fell from her hand. She wasn't dead, but in such a state of shock she could only fall to the ground and gingerly reach for the open wound at her neck.

Lonnie was deafened by the sound of the first shot that sent wooden splinters into his face and neck area. The second shot smashed the wooden fence inches from his head. He ducked and bolted through the open doors. Caudill had seen what happened, but for the first second or two Johns' own body had shielded Lonnie from Caudill's bullets. As Johns slipped to the ground Caudill saw an opportunity and snapped off two quick shots. She will never know how she missed him at such a short distance, but gunfights are like that. Her last view of Lonnie was of him running towards Ocean Highway.

Caudill screamed into her shoulder mic, "Officer down, officer down," and gave their location.

35
You Cover the Exits

At the sound of the first shot Brogan broke into a full run. The second shot came a split second later, closely followed by the voice of Officer Caudill screaming over the radio, "Officer down."

The two deputies who had been participating in the track also broke into a run, but were having trouble keeping up with Brogan who was in much better shape and unencumbered by all the leather-work of holsters, Tasers, batons, and handcuffs worn by the uniformed deputies. The K-9 man with the bloodhound followed them, but at a much slower pace, as bloodhounds are not built or trained for high-speed pursuits.

Brogan arrived at the garbage corral before anyone else and very quickly assessed the situation. Caudill was on the ground with Johns, attempting to stop the flow of blood with her own uniform shirt that she had ripped from her body and balled up to apply pressure on Johns' neck. Brogan had seen much death in his years as a cop and knew that Caudill's efforts were necessary, but futile.

Caudill looked up at Brogan without easing the pressure on Johns. Caudill's eyes were moist as she fought to hold back her tears. Without further explanation she told Brogan that the suspect had run toward Ocean Highway and was still armed with the knife. Caudill said, "Brogan, get that motherfucker!"

Brogan needed no further encouragement and knew he could do nothing to help Johns other than to get her killer. The two uniform deputies arrived panting heavily just as Brogan took off again towards Ocean Highway. Sucking it up, they tried to keep up with Brogan.

Brogan reached Ocean Highway and stopped. His head was on a swivel, scanning for any movement or indication as to which way Harris had gone. About a block to the south he saw what appeared to be a woman waving both hands above her head and motioning him towards her. Brogan ran as fast as he could to get to her.

When he arrived at her side she said, "He went in that building across the street. I saw him and he had a bag with him and he was holding a large knife. He went in the front door with some old man. He knocked the old man down and I don't know what happened after that."

Brogan looked towards the building. It was a five-story condo building called, Never Ending Summer Condominiums.

Strategic and tactical plans immediately began to form in Brogan's mind. He had been in this building several years ago, investigating a theft complaint from one of the residents. Interviews of multiple residents at that time gave him knowledge of the layout. He knew there were four condominiums per floor. Two facing towards the beach and two facing Ocean

Highway. All were privately owned and it was doubtful that many would be occupied at this time of the year. The front and back doors to the condominium were controlled by numerical keypads allowing entrance for the owners into a common lobby and hallway. There was a single elevator located in the center of the building that could be stopped at all five floors. Front and rear doors could be buzzed open from the owners' condos for guests. There was an internal phone system located outside both front and back doors. Guests would call the condo owners to be buzzed in. All the electrical boxes were on the rear of the building and the heating and air conditioning units were located on the roof.

There were also two interior emergency stairwells, one located in the front and one in the rear of the building. They offered access and egress from the building in the event of a fire or, more commonly, a broken elevator. On the fifth floor there was a single door leading to a flight of steps that opened onto the roof.

The two deputies drew up to Brogan and the woman. Brogan told one deputy to get her name and contact information and then come to the entrance of the condominium building across the street. He directed the other deputy to follow him. Brogan had purposely chosen the youngest and most fit deputy to come with him.

They sprinted across Ocean Highway and went directly to the entrance door. Looking through the glass doors they could see an elderly man sitting on the floor with his back against a wall. He looked dazed, but otherwise displayed no obvious signs of injury.

Brogan pounded on the glass door to draw the old man's attention. The elderly gentleman looked at Brogan with a puzzled look on his face. He appeared to try and focus. Brogan pounded some more and waived for the man to come to the door. The uniformed deputy stood right next to Brogan so there was no doubt they were the police. Brogan could see right through the building to the rear doors. They were closed and there was no movement in the hallway beyond the old man.

Slowly the old man tried to gain his footing, but was struggling to get to a standing position. He braced himself against the wall and used it to support himself as he moved towards the entrance.

For the first time Brogan noticed an aluminum walker in a far corner of the lobby and assumed it was the old man's main mode of transportation. It was further to the walker than it was to the front door so the elderly man wobbled his way towards Brogan. Arriving at the door, the old man threw his hand up against inner wall and apparently pressed a button releasing the auto-lock.

Brogan pushed through and told the deputy to stay with the man and radio for medical help. Brogan noticed a spreading red mark on the man's forehead where he had apparently hit his head or been struck. No wonder he was dazed. The elderly man used one hand to hold himself upright and his other hand and arm to point to the stairwell at the front of the building. Brogan knew Harris had gone that way and so would he.

Brogan told the deputy to position himself in the center of the hallway near the elevator and to shoot first if the suspect came out of either stairwell. Brogan reminded the deputy the suspect had killed at least three people including a police officer and had nothing to lose. He told the deputy that once the other deputy arrived and they had additional backup, to seal the bottom floor. He said, "I'll call you from the roof then begin to flush the suspect down towards you. Don't let anyone enter the elevator or the stairwells for fear of a crossfire situation." Brogan called the elevator to the lobby and covered the door with his gun as the doors slid open. It was empty. Brogan stepped inside and turned the elevator off. Now only the steps were left as a possible means of escape. Brogan stopped at the front stairwell and before entering turned to the deputy and said, "Cover the exits." The deputy nodded his understanding and drew his weapon from his holster. The deputy knew his focus should be mostly on the rear stairwell because he didn't think the suspect would get past Brogan under any circumstances. Brogan's steely blue eyes transmitted an unspoken message that this may end badly, but there was no doubt it would end now.

36
NOWHERE TO RUN

As Brogan entered the stairwell, all five senses were turned to the on position. He stopped and listened. He heard nothing. The steps were painted concrete with metal railings attached to the outer walls. The steps were fairly wide and there were small landings at each floor, with a metal door leading to that floor of condominiums. There was a small window in each door. The window revealed very little about what might be occurring in the hall. Each landing presented a possible ambush location. Solid inner walls provided a hiding place from which an assailant could leap. In this case, Lonnie Harris would have both the high ground and the possible momentum to carry out an attack, even if Brogan was lucky enough to snap off a shot.

Every cop is trained to know that a suspect with a knife can cross a room and deliver a fatal stab wound even if he has been shot. In this closed environment there would be virtually no time or distance to bring down the suspect before he would be on you.

Brogan would not rely solely on his gun. His martial arts

training and instincts would have to be enough to level the playing field. He crept up the first flight of steps keeping his back against the railing. As he neared the first landing he stopped and listened. Nothing.

Brogan crouched low and stepped onto the landing, pivoting at the same time to look up the next flight of steps. His gun was shoulder high and ready to fire. Nothing.

He noticed the landing doors all swung out and, on each landing, there was a recess holding a fire extinguisher. He removed the fire extinguisher and placed it against the door. If Harris tried to exit behind him the noise of the fire extinguisher being knocked over in this concrete tunnel would signal Lonnie's location. Brogan was sure the deputy in the lobby would take care of business if the suspect tried to flee behind Brogan. This also prevented the suspect from sneaking out and coming up behind Brogan.

This strategy and cautious advance was repeated four times before reaching the final set of steps leading to the fifth and top floor. Brogan had still heard nothing; each step increased the tension and likelihood an ambush would occur. Brogan had a clear view up at the fifth-floor landing and the door that would lead into the hallway. His gun never wavered; his concentration was set at a razor's edge.

He reached the fifth-floor landing and peeked through the window, but was unable to see more than a very small portion of the hallway. An attacker could easily be concealed on either side of the door ready to pounce. Brogan wasn't going to end this search by standing in the stairwell. He turned the door handle slowly until he felt the latch release. He pulled the door open about a foot and then immediately closed it with the weight of his shoulder holding it closed. He hoped if Harris were waiting to ambush him at the door, this would flush him into action. Nothing happened. Where was this asshole?

Brogan realized he should use his radio and call for backup. The shepherds could clear the roof and hallways. But this was personal because of Lynn Murphy and Officer Johns. This is what cops are paid to do. This is the calling that makes some people spend their adult lives carrying a gun, never being sure they would be going home from a work shift. This is the adrenaline rush that causes police and firemen to run into danger rather than away from it. It was time to earn his pay. Brogan jerked the door all the way open and breached the opening. Left—nothing. Right—nothing.

Had the old man been right about where Harris had gone? Had Lonnie found a way into one of the condominiums or escaped out the back door before Brogan and the deputy made it to the building?

There were six doors on this floor. Brogan had just come through one. Four more were entrances to condominiums and the sixth was the door leading to the roof. Brogan went there first and could see by the doorframe that this particular door swung in. Knowing this door would be locked and only accessible by maintenance personnel, Brogan examined the doorknob and lock closely. There it was – the faint outline of a footprint. Lonnie Harris had kicked this door open to gain access to the roof. This was a five-story building, so this was it. No place to run!

Brogan pushed the door open. Surprisingly, the hinges were well oiled and the door moved silently. An additional fifteen steps led to a metal door that would surely open to the roof. There was no landing at the top of the steps, so the door would swing out.

Brogan checked his watch. The time had passed quickly and it was approaching 6:30 a.m. On the roof the light of a new day would just be taking hold. The problem was that Brogan would be moving from a lighted stairwell into the relative darkness of a new dawn. It would take seconds for his eyes to adjust and he didn't have seconds. Without hesitation, Brogan reached up and stuck the butt of his gun between the metal screening that protected the bulb. A slight tap and the bulb broke and the stairwell was thrown into darkness. Not total darkness as there was light leaking in from around the metal door that separated him from the roof. Brogan's eyes adjusted to the dim lighting and he was ready to go out on the roof and confront the killer that had put his city in a state of fear and lockdown.

The metal door had no locking mechanism and was held closed from the inside by a sliding bolt that was disengaged, reaffirming that Harris had passed this way.

Brogan gently pushed against the metal door and as it swung open he was able to look through the crack on the hinged side and see that no one was on that side. He ducked quickly through the access with his gun focused on the non-hinged side. Brogan's head swiveled left to right and realized the lighting from nearby buildings was adding light to the natural sunrise.

Brogan was looking at twenty air handling units mounted on the roof, plus other machinery he could not immediately identify. There were also several antennas and cables whose purpose were unknown to Brogan. Around the entire circumference of the roof there was a very low wall, maybe thirty-six inches high. The surface of the roof was black tar paper covered with pea-sized gravel. There were plenty of places to hide, but no place to escape.

A five-gallon can filled with sand sat near the door. Apparently, workers had used it as an ashtray. Brogan moved the can in front of the door while maintaining a watch on his surroundings.

Brogan then began to stalk his unseen prey. Gun up and ready. He positioned himself in such a way that Harris would not be able to access the rooftop door without becoming a target. The heating/air-conditioning units were set in five groups of four, corresponding with the number of floors and number of condo units. Each unit had enough room around it for maintenance and each was mounted on small metal feet that allowed approximately one or two inches of space under each unit. Brogan would have to lie down to see under the units. He was not inclined to do that and he doubted the current lighting conditions would allow him to see much of anything anyway.

Without warning, Lonnie suddenly rose from behind one of the units, approximately twenty feet from where Brogan stood. Lonnie held his hands down by his sides and the unit hid them.

Brogan brought the front and rear of his gun's sights onto his target. Center mass of Lonnie's body was the target. In a calm and quiet voice Brogan said, "Lonnie it's over. Let me see your hands."

Lonnie lifted his hands so Brogan could see the knife in one and the canvas bag in the other. Brogan ordered Lonnie to place the knife and the bag on the unit and to move out into the open. Lonnie put the bag on the unit, but retained the knife and moved from behind the unit so there was nothing but space between him and Brogan.

Lonnie said, "I listened to you last time and you fucked me

over and sent me to jail. I came back to make things right. I killed that bitch on the beach because she was part of it. She worked in the courtroom where they decided I should be tried as an adult. She wasn't the same lady, but she was doing the same shit. Becky had to die to keep my secret. I told her I was here to take care of some stuff and she couldn't be trusted." Lonnie's voice became louder as he baited Brogan to act. "Your girlfriend has some pretty nice tits, doesn't she? If you had given me a little time with her she would have forgotten all about you." Brogan said nothing.

Lonnie tried again. "Is that lady cop dead? Did you train her Brogan? You did, didn't you? That's why she fucked up and got herself killed." Brogan said nothing. "You want me Brogan? Come and get me." Brogan said nothing.

Suicide by cop flashed in Brogan's mind. Not a bad idea, but not the way this was going to end.

Lonnie saw the change in Brogan, saw his steel blue eyes had turned to flint. Lonnie knew he had crossed a line and waited for the impact of the bullets that would end his miserable life. The shots never came. Instead Lonnie was amazed to see Brogan reholster his weapon and snap the safety strap to secure it.

Lonnie also experienced a change. He went from being resigned to die in a hail of bullets to reverting to the hunter. What did this old cop think he was doing? Did he expect Lonnie to lay down his knife and surrender quietly? Whatever he thought it was clear he had his head up his ass. Lonnie was going to hurt this guy bad, kill him and then throw his body off the roof.

Lonnie had no delusion of escape as he was sure there was an army of cops waiting downstairs for him, but if he killed

Brogan, Lonnie Harris would be legendary for his crimes and be forever remembered in the history of this town.

Lonnie edged forward, closing the distance between him and Brogan. Neither spoke as they locked eyes. Lonnie held the KA-BAR in his right hand and slightly away from his body. The blade was pointed up.

As the distance shrank between them, Brogan calmed himself and went to a place where everything slowed down and his senses gave way to his training.

Lonnie moved quickly forward and slashed wildly at Brogan seeking to gut him. Brogan stepped back and to his left, putting himself behind the knife hand. Brogan threw a right-hand punch and drove his fist into the side of Lonnie's head. The blow had intentionally been pulled at the last second so it merely stunned Lonnie and he staggered a little before regaining his balance, turning again to face Brogan. Lonnie shifted the knife in his hand and came again with the intent to strike down, as he had done with the female police officer. Brogan stepped inside and parried the knife away. He then delivered a right-hand strike to Lonnie's nose before withdrawing and moving again out of Lonnie's reach.

Lonnie back peddled away from Brogan, clearly stunned by the punch to the nose that hurt like hell and was bleeding profusely. Still on his feet and now blinded by anger, he charged wildly at Brogan, who performed a perfect spinning kick that put Lonnie on his ass. He again withdrew to await Lonnie's next move.

Tears of pain were streaming down Lonnie's face. They mixed with the blood and snot flowing freely from his broken nose. He regained his feet and moved back a few more steps to regroup. This time Brogan came to him and then stopped a few steps out of Lonnie's reach. Lonnie unleashed a stream of profanities and threats toward Brogan who said nothing.

Brogan's continued silence was more damaging to Lonnie's psychic than all the blows he had received. Rage surfaced again and removed the last trace of any commonsense Lonnie possessed. Lonnie screamed, "Fuck you Brogan, I'm going to kill you." He charged forward with his arms out from his sides as if to embrace, encircle, or tackle Brogan.

Brogan executed a front thrust kick, catching Lonnie squarely in the chest and driving him backwards. Lonnie had completely ignored the fact that all his backing up had taken him dangerously close to the rooftop wall. The kick drove him to the wall and it caught him just below his butt. Lonnie felt himself falling backwards and his arms pinwheeled, trying to regain his balance. His eyes met Brogan's and for the first time Brogan spoke, "No, fuck you Lonnie. The women you killed are screaming for justice. Now they have it."

Lonnie fell over the wall screaming all the way to the concrete apron that awaited his arrival, clutching the KA-BAR all the way to the ground. The impact shattered most of his bones. His grip loosened and the knife clattered a few inches from his hand.

Brogan stared out over the skyline of Sandpiper and could already anticipate the relief that would spread throughout the city now that Harris was dead. Brogan lifted his portable radio and called the officers below advising them the suspect was down and the building was secure. Justice had been done and Brogan would rest well tonight.

On the concrete below, Lonnie's blood pooled around his body, engulfing the knife, adding his blood to that of his victims. This had begun with extreme violence and now it had ended the same way.

37
THE AFTERMATH

Things had been hectic for several days. The news media was going crazy with the story of a "mad dog killer" who had been brought down by a courageous detective. The public couldn't get enough of the story.

The deceased were being mourned in both Maryland and Pennsylvania. Distraught families and friends were planning funerals and struggling to deal with the emptiness they found in their lives. All agreed that the death of the killer had brought them some measure of closure, but nothing would replace those they had lost.

The mayor and chief of police were both congratulated for their handling of the circumstances and were guaranteed continued employment and adoration from a grateful constituency. Their faith in Brogan had been bolstered once again and he would remain unquestionably their lead guy in all things criminal.

The State Police and State's attorney's office were handling the death investigation of Lonnie Harris, but it was clear already that their findings would show that Brogan had acted appropriately under extremely dangerous circumstances. The fact that Brogan had not shot Harris, but rather decided to physically subdue him, was the only area that seemed to leave some doubt as to Brogan's handling of the situation. Everyone agreed that under similar circumstances they would have shot Harris.

The physical evidence matching the knife to the wounds of all the victims and the eyewitness testimony of Officer Caudill would have been damning in a court trial. Taxpayers and victim's families were spared the cost and hardships of a trial by the actions of Detective Brogan.

Inmate Snelling had his sentenced reduced and was glad Lonnie had gotten his due for trying to fuck him over.

Officer Caudill was placed on paid administrative leave, pending an internal investigation into the facts leading to officer Johns death. The investigation would continue, but Caudill had already concluded that the death of Johns fell squarely on her shoulders and had submitted her resignation. She believed she could no longer bear the responsibility for the life and death decisions made by police officers.

Brogan had been placed on paid administrative leave while the investigation into his actions was being conducted. He had used the time off to reunite with Lynn Murphy. Because she was part of the story, she had also been given time off.

Brogan and Murphy had been locked away in a hotel room just outside of DC for the better part of two days. Meals were being ordered from the room-service menu. Brogan knew this was another stress reliever for both of them and that this relationship would probably never advance more than it already had. Lonnie Harris had been right about only one thing. Lynn Murphy did have great tits.

Three murders in a summer resort in the dead of winter had caught the eye of the national media as well.

In a distant city, a young woman watched the news coverage and was unable to stop the tears that ran over the faded scars on her face. For the first time in over ten years she felt safe. She whispered to herself, "Rot in hell Lonnie Harris."

ACKNOWLEDGEMENTS

M y wife has been on me for as long as I've known her to write a book. We didn't marry until after my State Police career was over, but she met all the players, heard all the stories, and thought I had the ability to tell a tale.

Thanks, Tobie for believing in me and pushing me to tell this story. I had fun doing it and had encouragement from a lot of people. Everybody wanted to be in the book and in one way or another most of them are in there somewhere.

While I had no intention of publishing this book, Tobie is already planning to get us bit parts when the movie is made.

A special thanks to all my friends who previewed the book and provided positive feedback. Ricky Haynes is a proofreader extraordinaire. When editor Bill Cecil edited the book, he showed me I still had a lot of work to do. After the final edit I went back and added over three thousand words. Thanks Bill for the words of encouragement and help bringing this project across the finish line.

Many may say, it's obvious that Sandpiper is Ocean City, MD. I have always loved Ocean City and now make it my home. I would not sully the name of the city I love, so Brogan will forever patrol the streets of Sandpiper.

Brogan says he has a few other case stories that may need telling. He's a bit of a hound dog, so you never know.